Self-Published Kindling:
Memoirs of a Homeless Bookstore Owner

by Mik Everett

For everyone who has shared their story

One

Everyone keeps telling me to write a book about this. I have a canned response to dish out: I'm working on a poetry manuscript instead of a novel; I'm going to publish a book of *poetry* about this. I have a very neat logic behind it with which no literary enthusiast can argue: I write poetry instead because it's easier to write when you live like I do. Easier than a novel, anyway. At night when I can't sleep, I string verses together, memorizing them a line at a time. (I say it craftily like that. People appreciate the metaphor. They think it makes me a poet.) I rework each stanza over and over and over, until I can recite them in order like beads on a chain. By the time a poem is complete, by the time each word is perfect, I have it memorized. Later, the next morning or three days later or whenever, when I go to the library to use the computer, when I have a chance to sit down with my laptop, whatever, I unstring each bead, each memorized stanza, onto the page. My poems appear on the paper exactly as they have all the times I turned them over and over again in my head. I have weighed each stanza, charting their size again and again: on the bus as city blocks roll past, against the wall where I wait in line at the food pantry, in my lap while I wait for a God with a clipboard to call my name in an office. My poems fit everywhere I go.

You can't do that with prose; or it's not as easy, anyway. Poetry is neatly compartmentalized for memorization. Prose, on the other hand, is not a polymer. It's harder to memorize unstrung sentences, anecdotes with words that don't match up in their sound. Some people memorize stories like jokes; the punchlines are the beads on their strings. But assonance and consonance make it easier for me. That's why I'm writing poetry instead of a novel.

People nod thoughtfully when I tell them this. Yes, this makes so much sense, they say. They regard me like a misfortuned craftsman, making the best of my situation. Oh, yes, she has the right idea. She has a plan.

It's funny how people's opinions of you can differ when they think you have a plan.

But it's sort of a lie. It is true that poetry is easier to memorize when I don't have anywhere to write. But it's a clumsy excuse and I breathe a sigh of relief each time someone buys it. My reason for not writing a book is a little more sinister than that; Poetry doesn't require a plot. Even a whole book of poems is permitted to be plotless; each poem is a vignette and the collection is a work of art. But novels are different; they require a plot. And plot requires causation. And there is no causation here. There is no reason for this. It just is.

I decided, against my prior (better) judgements, that I *would* write a book, during Open Mic Night at our bookstore last Thursday. John and I had owned the bookstore for about eight months, and had been homeless for two. A bright young poet and his literary agent were in attendance; they were both seventeen years old and had just graduated from high school. The poet's name was Dustin, and I don't remember his literary agent's name. Dustin was the sort of kid who always followed the rules, and if he didn't like the rules, he would change them. Dustin had published his first book of poetry-- a real, full-length book of poetry, like I am writing now-- when he was fourteen. He says that the book is unfamiliar to him now because the poems reflect how he felt at fourteen and he can't relate to them much now. A publisher picked out the cover art and formatting. He gave birth to what is now a stranger in his hands. At seventeen, Dustin edits a literary magazine with a few other enthusiasts, one of whom is a fairly prestigious underground-lit guru of New Jersey. Dustin's literary agent is a tall, lanky boy, whose only indicator that he has passed puberty is his height of over six feet. He purchased a P.O. box for his occupation and sends letters to publishers in New York, claiming that Dustin has a variety of talents including the handcrafting of felt hats. His hope is that he may be ridiculous enough to catch someone's attention. I don't much care for the modern traditional publishing industry but I wish them well.

As I said, that Thursday was Dustin's last day of high school. We were asking him about his plans for the future-- You know, the typical inspection to which the adult populace are wont to subject new graduates.

"Actually, I'm going to put off college, for now. I'm going to be traveling around starting in August. I'm working for the summer and then a couple of buddies and I are just going to, you know, drive around and sleep on people's couches and stuff."

"How is your mom taking it?" John asked. We knew his mother pretty well, as she was an advocate for the homeless. She didn't know that we were homeless; only that we were vocal supporters of her organization.

The literary agent dissolved into snickers at John's question. "She, ah, doesn't know yet," Dustin said.

"Ohh. I'm glad you told us that so we don't accidentally out you," I said.

"I'm waiting for the right time. I need to give her enough time to, like, adjust to it, but I don't want to tell her now because we're not leaving till August and I don't want to have to spend all summer with her trying to convince me not to go."

"You can always do college after your adventure," John suggested.

"Yeah, I know, and I know she wants me to go to college, but I think the main thing is she'll also worry about me, like, sleeping on people's couches and stuff."

John and I exchanged a glance. "You know, we traveled around a lot for a while," I said.

"Oh, really?" Dustin asked, leaning forward in his seat. "Where at? When?"

"Last summer," John said. "We mostly just drove up and down the Rockies until we found a place we wanted to stay. That's how we wound up here."

"It was a little different because we couldn't exactly couch-surf, you know, with kids," I said.

"Ohhh, right."

"Like, no one wants a whole family crashing in their living room."

"We mostly just camped and stuff," John added.

"That's pretty cool," Dustin nodded, and pretty soon, he and his literary agent left for another engagement, probably a party.

"I wish we could have told him about our visitor last night," I told John while we cleaned up after the event.

"Yeah, but I couldn't figure out how to tell him without, you know, giving it away. Where we live."

"Yeah. I also wish we could have warned him."

John nodded and didn't say anything else.

We wish we could warn him that this isn't any fun at all. But he's seventeen years old and he's already done everything else, so why not travel the country with no plan at all. And I mean that respectfully. He really has done everything else. He is a very well-respected and talented poet.

Instead of warning Dustin, I decided I would write a book, after all.

I'll tell *you* about our visitor, but first I have to explain where we live. The town of Longmont, Colorado, is a smallish town of 85,000 people; it is the more conservative and provincial cousin of Boulder. It's twenty minutes north of the bohemian bourgeoise and Naropa University and the Jack Kerouac School of Disembodied Poets. Kerouac himself lounged under a tree in front of a gas station in Longmont, in *On the Road*, and Dustin has a poem about that tree that isn't there any more. It's in his book he published at fourteen. I told you he was talented.

Anyway, we might have done better in Boulder, where people respect art and stuff-- and, more importantly, buy it. Longmont likes to pretend that it is progressive, but it is only an image; and order and budget will not be sacrificed for this image. We had a hard time marketing our store to Longmont residents, and we failed to pay our rent a few times. The bookstore survived, but we were evicted from our apartment.

Right now we live in a broken-down motorhome in a Wal-Mart parking lot. This is how we came to meet our visitor about whom I wanted to tell Dustin.

Last Monday, John had to work late at the liquor store, and the kids and I were in town so that I could take a shower. I had a job interview Tuesday, so I paid a dollar for a shower at the rec center while John played with the kids at the park. Then he went to work and the kids and I played at the park for a while, but Lyric threw sand at another kid and Sophie threw a tantrum, so we left. It was a two-mile walk up Main Street from Roosevelt Park to the Wal-Mart at Highway 66. It was very sunny and hot, even that late in the day, and we crossed the highway at the intersection and dodged honking wayward jeeps and were almost cooked on the black asphalt from the sideways heat of sunset. We tramped through some wildflowers towards a little section of the parking lot, furthest away from the Wal-Mart, nestled between a fast-food restaurant and a propane refill center. In this alcove of asphalt, there were probably six motorhomes parked; an inexplicable motorboat; two camper-trailers with no trucks in sight; and four or five cars that people were obviously living out of. Most had blankets up in the windows. One campsite was comprised of two vans parked next to each other with their doors open, and a sort of blanket-fort tunnel connecting the two. Some cars had a group of shopping carts parked outside, used as extra storage space so that the inhabitants would have room to sleep in their cars.

Our motorhome wasn't here. It was on the other side of Wal-Mart, to the north, by the automotive center. We had towed it there because we figured that if anyone told us to move it, we could tell them that it didn't run (true) and we had brought it to Wal-Mart to see if they could repair it for us (false) and that once we found out Wal-Mart doesn't repair motorhomes (true), we were looking for a way to get it towed elsewhere (sort of true but not really). We also parked it there because, at the time, we didn't know about the motorhome community on the west side of Wal-Mart.

Our Chevy pick-up was also in the automotive parking lot to the north of Wal-Mart, near our motorhome, because the power steering belt came off when we were trying to go home Sunday night. We *did* pay to have the truck towed there for repairs, for real. But it turned out Wal-Mart doesn't do belt installations, either.

The north side of Wal-Mart wasn't a good location. It was too close to the building and we could only come to the motorhome after dark, for fear someone would see us. We also were kept up all night by floodlights and workers welding and running chainsaws outside. I have no idea what the workers were constructing; shelving, perhaps. And there was a train that ran to the north of Wal-Mart, and the motorhome shook whenever the train went by.

I wanted to move; I also figured that someone in the west parking lot probably knew something about motorhomes. Ever since I noticed the gathering of motorhomes in the west lot, I kept telling John that one of these days I was going to go make friends with them and see if any of them knew a thing or two about motorhomes. John would say okay but I knew he thought I was just talking. To him, I still was a timid, bookish girl with social anxiety and a competitive complex; not the type to go make friends in a shanty-town.

But that Monday evening, dragging a child on each hand, I made my way to the center of the lot and looked around at the motorhomes around me. I didn't know which were occupied. I spied an old man in the cab of a truck with a slide-in camper in the back; on the other side of me, another man exited his motorhome, threw a trash bag into the dump truck parked next to his motorhome, and went back inside. I weighed my options.

I could see the second man in his motorhome through his back window, because his curtains were drawn open. I waved to him, and he came out of the motorhome. He was a large man, both in his stomach and in his upper body.

"Hey..." I started as he came close enough to hear me. "Do you know anything about RV's?"

He looked at me sideways. "Sure," he said.

"Well, we've been living in a broken-down motorhome on the other side of Wal-Mart and I just came over here because I figure someone over here knows something about motorhomes and might be able to help me and I don't have a lot of money to pay for help but I can pay you in weed."

The man waved my comment away. "Oh no, I'm on probation anyway," he said in a thick Southern accent. "but I'll take a look at it. You don't got to pay me nothing. Say, your kids look like they could use some cheesecake. Come on in." He held open the door to his motorhome. The kids clambered in without waiting for a response from me, and I followed them. The motorhome was neatly-kept, except for a pile of dishes in the sink. I felt a pang of jealousy; we didn't have running water because the water pump in our motorhome was powered by electricity. Or would be, if we had any electricity. The kids sat down at the table, and the man set a miniature New York cheesecake from Wal-Mart down in front of them.

"I don't got a lot of forks," he said. "Can you kids use your hands?"

"No," Lyric said, but I said, "Yes, you can. Just hold onto the crust." The man insisted that I have some, too, but I declined, flushed with embarrassment.

"So tell me about what's wrong with your motorhome," the man drawled, but just as I started to explain, his cell phone rang.

"Hold on a sec," he said, and the kids munched away at their cheesecake. "No, no, I've got a job up in Estes Park tomorrow. I've got a lot going on right now. I told you to come by yesterday because I didn't have a job yesterday. I can't come out tomorrow."

"Where's the bed at?" Lyric asked, peering around the motorhome.

"I bet this table turns into a bed," I said. "What do you think?"

"The world does not revolve around Raymond," the man growled into the phone. "I got a friend here I need to help. You're gonna have to wait till I have a day again. I can't set everything down just because you couldn't come out yesterday." He hung up the phone and turned his attention to me.

I told him all about our bad luck buying the motorhome and the myriad of possible problems, mostly electrical. "Well, I just happen to be an electrician," he said. "Let's go take a look at that thing."

Dusk was upon us as we circumnavigated the giant expanse of the Wal-Mart parking lot. The kids, always hungry for attention, jostled to hold our new friend's hands. "I got a lot of jobs I'm workin' on, actually. I came up here from Springs this winter with only the clothes on my back. Nothin' but the clothes on my back. I'm doin' pretty well for myself now. Got the RV, got the truck. Was operatin' a snow-shovelin' business during the winter. I had about sixty homeless people employed for me, shovelin' snow everywhere."

"I can respect that," I said.

"Now I'm working as a ranch hand outside of Longmont, and it's paying pretty good. Using that for operatin' capital so I can start a tree-trimming business, now that there ain't snow any more."

"You sound very entrepreneurial," I said.

"Sure am," he said. "Truth is, this is a new life for me. I came up to Longmont to start a new life. Had to get out of Springs. Truth is, your kids is holdin' hands with a Hell's Angel." He paused for me to react. I made some respectfully impressed platitudes. "I'm retired from that life now, but I was pretty well up. I can walk into any Hell's Angels chapter in America and the only person higher up than me is the president of that chapter."

I debated telling our new friend that John might have a hit out on him by the Hell's Angels, but I decided against it. John's had custody of Lyric since Lyric was about a year old, because Lyric's mother couldn't care for him any more due to meth addiction. She'd been using since before Lyric was born, and though John swore up and down that she'd been clean during her pregnancy, you didn't have to be around Lyric long to understand that his father was gullible and his mother was a liar as well as a meth addict. Lyric's maternal grandmother, an ex-biker with a back injury, had mostly cared for Lyric as a baby, due to his mother's addiction and John's absence. When her back got too bad and she couldn't care for Lyric anymore either, John stepped up. He'd been raising Lyric by himself for about six months when we'd started dating, back when we lived in Wichita, and on weekends he still took Lyric out to a little town in Western Kansas to see Lyric's maternal grandmother. But with Lyric's mother still hanging around and smoking in the house, the environment was toxic both figuratively and literally, and John moved us out here to Colorado without telling Lyric's mother or grandmother or letting them say goodbye. We suspected that the grandmother was probably pretty angry. She had been in relationships with some Hell's Angels during her life, and we could reasonably assume that if she still knew any, they'd be trying to find us.

Instead, I told our new Hell's Angel friend all about running a bookstore, about how we had the opportunity to open a shop and went for it, and how we didn't have very much capital but it was an inexpensive business and we wanted so badly for it to work.

"Well, see, I'm also a writer," the Hell's Angel said. "I used to be pretty popular in my day. Had a lot of popular stories on MySpace. I been thinkin' about turning them into a book. Been thinkin' about self-publishing."

"No kidding!" I exclaimed. "I work in self-publishing! That's what we do at our bookstore. We carry self-published books and sometimes we help authors publish them."

"That's great. That's really great. When I get it finished I'll talk to you!"

"Yeah, let me know if I can help at all. I'd love to help you get it published. I can do that for you for taking a look at the motorhome." And I handed him a business card from my purse.

"That's be just great. That would be wonderful." He pocketed the card.

I was really happy, because I hated asking a favor without having a way of paying it back. I'd been counting on being able to use my supply of medical marijuana as collateral, and since that had fallen through, I was relieved to have a back-up.

We arrived at the motorhome and our dog, Rigby, greeted us with a wagging tail and a grin. It's incredible how you can leave a dog all day and it still loves you when you come home. I set the kids up in John's and my bed, in the bunk above the dashboard, so that our new friend could get to the electrical stuff, most of which was under the kids' beds. Rigby darted in and out of the motorhome while our friend checked out the auxiliary battery underneath Lyric's bed.

"Oh. See, here's the problem. This hooks up to a marine battery, and you don't got a marine battery here. You got an automotive battery."

"There's another one somewhere," I said, and I looked all over the motorhome. I looked in the bath tub, which contained a spare tire, a license plate, and a trash can, but not a battery. I finally located it in the dark, against the wall by the busted oven.

"It's an automotive battery too. I think we can rig this up but we gotta see if it can hold a charge first. What you gotta do is take these in to Wal-Mart and see if they have a charge."

"They'll just do that?"

"Yeah, sure, any automotive place will do that. You just take it in and they'll tell you whether or not it has a charge."

He exited the motorhome and peered underneath, where the electrical wiring supposedly hooked up to the propane tank and an outlet, but it was too dark to see much and of course we didn't have lights.

"I'm just gonna have to map this all out in the daylight," he said. "Ain't nothin' I can do until it gets light."

"Oh, I understand," I insisted. "I didn't expect you to do anything tonight anyway. I just wanted to see if anyone knew anything about motorhomes."

"You want me to tow you over to the other side of Wal-Mart? You're not comfortable over here, are you?"

I shook my head, smiling nervously.

"Listen, as soon as your husband gets home from work, you come wake me up. I don't care what time it is. You come wake me up and I'll get my one-ton out here and we'll get this thing towed."

With a promise that I would wake him up when John came home, and that I would help him publish his book, our friend left. I put the kids to bed and resolved to stay awake till John got home, but I was comfortably asleep when he softly crept into the motorhome.

"Hi," I said, sitting up and rubbing my eyes.

"Hi," he whispered back, taking off his shoes.

"A Hell's Angel gave the kids some cheesecake," I said, and I told John everything my new friend had told me. But we decided it was too late and we were too tired to move the motorhome that night, so we curled up together in an innocent embrace.

"I had a daydream that he'd be able to fix it easy and you'd come home to the lights on and everything working," I confessed to him as we drifted off to sleep.

In the morning, I went to go see our friend about a tow, but his truck was gone and no one answered my knock on the motorhome door, so I surmised that he had already left for work.

It was Wednesday night before we saw him again; my friend Alex gave us a ride home from the shop after work, and I asked her to enter on the west side of the parking lot by the shanty-town so we could see if our friend was home. Both his Dodge El Dorado motorhome and his black one-ton truck were parked there, so she let us out beside his motorhome. The truck was the chassis of a pick-up truck, but seemed to have a hand-built wooden dump truck on the back. I'm not sure what the frame was. About a dozen snow shovels peeked over the edge of the wooden bed.

I knocked on the door of the motorhome, a little concerned that our new friend would think I was flakey. But when he saw it was me at the door, he broke into a grin.

"Well, come on in! Where y'all been? I came to check on you yesterday but y'all weren't home."

He was shirtless and held open the door for us, and his motorhome was in disarray compared to its neatness on Monday. The kitchen table was folded out into an unmade bed with dark green sheets.

"I'm sorry, John got home so late on Monday that I was already asleep and he didn't want to wake me up. I'm sorry I missed you."

"Aw, that's all right. And you must be John. I'm Axel."

They shook hands, and I was relieved to finally know our friend's name-- I was afraid that my social ineptitude would be made obvious when I was forced to make introductions.

"Let me put a shirt on real fast, and then I'll get my one-ton out there and give you guys a tow."

We all piled back out of the motorhome, and were met by a neat woman in a pants-suit carrying a clipboard. My heart rose to my throat.

"Excuse me. Do you know if there's anyone in this RV who needs a meal?"

"Sure! We'll take some!" I said excitedly, relieved she wasn't an employee of either Wal-Mart or the city of Longmont. Actually, she was from the organization for which Dustin's

mother worked: Homeless Outreach Providing Encouragement, or
H.O.P.E. I did have a can of chicken in my backpack and stale
bagels from the food pantry, and we had planned on eating that
for dinner-- Cold, with everyone sharing one fork. She led me to a
minivan on the other side of Axel's motorhome; the trunk of the
minivan was full of brown paper bags. These meals undoubtably
contained something better than cold chicken, I thought.

The woman counted out six for me, then had me sign my
name on her clipboard. "Just your first name's okay," she said.
"Do you need a jacket or anything?" She eyed my tank top and
skirt. It was getting chilly in the darkening evening.

"Nah, I got a jacket in the truck. Thank you!"

Axel was on the phone when I returned from the van. The
doors to his truck were open, and John was helping the kids into
the passenger seat.

"You ride with the kids," he said. "I'll walk and meet you
there. You should be staying off your foot."

I climbed in with the kids, clutching six brown paper bags,
and Axel climbed in the driver's seat, still on the phone.

"No, not tomorrow, I got to meet my probation officer.
And I'm working on the ranch. We got to get some capital
together, so we can get the saws and stuff. Ya know? I want to
look professional. This is gonna be good for us if we can look
professional."

We drove across the Wal-Mart parking lot, and as we
neared the motorhome, I watched John, who had a head-start on
us, cross the grassy knoll by our motorhome. On the hill, next to a
hitch-hiking backpack and a sleeping bag bundle, perched a kid in
a denim vest.

"I got recommended to the Parks Board in Estes Park,"
Axel told me proudly when he hung up the phone. I congratulated
him, and he put the truck in park and hopped out to hook up the
tow chains. I got out of the truck, too, and waited patiently for
John to finish discussing the length of the tow chains with Axel.
Rigby ran back and forth, excited to be free from the motorhome.

"Well, will you be able to stop without hitting me?" Axel asked.

"I think so," John said with the intonation of a question, totally unsure of his response. Axel gave the chains a shake.

"Did you talk to that kid over there?" I asked.

"What?" John said. Of course he had no reason to, but he hardly ever passed up a hitch-hiker or panhandler without giving them something; if he had no money, he might give them a ride or a roach. If he had neither, he might at least give a minute of his time, just to ask how they were doing or listen to their story, so I had thought he might've talked to the kid.

"I'm gonna go offer him a meal if that's okay," I said. John nodded without looking up from the tow chains.

"Hey," I said to the kid. He looked up from his book and blew out a cloud of smoke. He had olive skin and brown, curly hair that wasn't quite to his shoulders. It was hard for me to tell if he was very stocky, or simply wearing a lot of clothing. His jeans had vertical holes ripped in the knees, so that not just his knobby knees, but most of his tanned calves were exposed as well. "The homeless outreach people just came by on the other side of Wal-Mart and they gave us six meals and we only have four people so I was wondering if you want one."

"Well, I got food, but if you don't need it..." He trailed off, playing with the white bandana around his neck. I thought of our can of cold chicken and handed him the paper bag. "What people did you say it was?"

"Some homeless outreach people. I guess they come around on the other side, where the motorhomes are parked, every evening to see if anyone needs anything."

"I won't be here for long," the boy said. "I got some friends coming down from Seattle in a couple of days and we're gonna ride to New Mexico. Just waiting around till then. You want some of this?" He passed me a red joint, now not much more than a roach, and I took a hit and left him and went back to the truck where John and Axel were still messing with the tow cables.

"He's just homeless for a couple days. He's got friends coming to pick him up next week," I said.

"Does he have somewhere to sleep tonight?" John asked.

"He had a sleeping bag."

"You should go offer him a bed in our motorhome."

"No! He'll think I'm hitting on him. His stuff's pretty good though, I had one hit and I'm already baked."

"Well, would you be okay with giving him a bed tonight?"

"Sure, but you go ask him... Mention that I'm your girlfriend!" I added as John walked off. I got back in Axel's truck with the kids and watched out the window as John and the hitch-hiking boy exchanged words. The boy got up, picked up his pack, and I watched in the rear-view mirror as he got in the motorhome with John and Rigby.

Axel started the truck and we took off with a jerk. He turned to me and winked. "He'll get the hang of it," he said, meaning John. I grinned, thinking of all the times I'd been behind the wheel of the dead motorhome, heart pounding while John towed in the truck. The brakes were bad and stopping before I hit the truck was always a nerve-wracking experience that required balancing myself on the steering wheel while I put my full body's weight down on the brake pedal.

Axel pulled the motorhome through the Wal-Mart parking lot and into the alcove, then parked us between a camper trailer and the motorboat. We were in the next aisle after Axel's Dodge El Dorado, about even with it. His was parked at the north edge of the alcove, which was about five aisles wide and maybe ten parking spaces deep. I helped the children down from Axel's truck and set them on the rear bumper of our motorhome to eat their sack lunches while John and Axel unhooked the tow chains. The paper sacks each contained a meat-and-cheese sandwich, in various combinations, and a bag of chips. They all had two or three other items: A clementine, a cookie, crackers, a pudding cup, or a fruit cup. I told the kids to eat their sandwiches to get their cookies, and left them to try to help with the motorhome.

Axel was plugging his generator into our motorhome's outlet, and John and I flipped switches and breakers inside, trying to ascertain if anything electrical was working. Nothing turned on. I went back and forth between helping with the switches and trying to coral the children, who were climbing all over the bumper and not eating their sandwiches at all. I was eager to eat mine, very nearly starving after two months of food-pantry stale bread for virtually every meal, but wanted to wait till the work was done so I could sit down and eat with John. The man from the camper trailer next to ours came out and told John several times that he should build a dog run, but everyone ignored him and eventually he went back inside. His name was Billy and he had a pregnant wife.

Everyone gave up on the electricity because Axel's generator blew, so I sent the children inside and put the movie *Peter Pan* on the laptop for them to watch. I had charged the laptop at work so they could watch a movie, which we did two or three times a week. Sophie had ripped half of her sandwich up and thrown it on the ground, and Rigby found it and ate it, so I gave Rigby the other half of her sandwich and told Sophie she wouldn't be having anything else to eat. Once the children were engrossed in the movie, John and I and our hitch-hiking friend stepped out to smoke a bowl.

"Don't use too much," John said as I broke up the weed. "I need to have some left to pay the guy that's coming to fix the truck tomorrow."

Our new friend offered to roll us a joint with his weed, and we happily accepted. He had watermelon-flavored rolling papers, which is why they were red.

Outside the motorhome, we smoked and avoided the puddle under Billy's camper trailer, which was expanding into the space between his camper and ours. It seemed his sewage drain was open. I hoped it was just grey water from the sink and shower, but I couldn't be sure. John and our visitor compared cops around America.

"In New Jersey, where I'm from, they don't have

misdemeanors any more. Except, like, moving violations. Everything's a felony. Weed is a felony."

"Cops suck in Wichita. We're from Wichita"

"Is that the capital of Kansas?" the hitch-hiker asked.

"No, Topeka is. But Wichita is bigger. You don't ever want to go to Topeka," John said.

"Wichita's the biggest city in Kansas, but the problem is, it has corruption problems like in Chicago and New Orleans," I said. "Wichita's tiny, compared to them. But their police are just as bad," I said.

"Jesus," he said.

"If you're driving a car with Colorado tags, they'll box you into a parking lot so you can't leave. No fucking probable cause or anything. Just that you're from Colorado. And they won't give you a badge number or anything."

"They're like that in California, but Arizona is the worst. I was down there with some buddies and they fucking tore our car apart."

"Whaaaat?" John exclaimed. "Why? They thought you were smuggling drugs?"

"No, they thought we were smuggling people. I mean, we're obviously gringos, but they stop us and tear the car apart. They were really cool about it."

John laughed again. "After they tore your car apart."

"Yeah, and we even had a box of pieces on us, I don't know how the dog missed it. But later I asked one of the guys, I was like, 'What does your job consist of?' And he was like, 'Pretty much just jumping out at people from behind bushes with a flashlight.'"

"I want that to be my job," John said, even though I knew he really didn't. Maybe the jumping-out-with-a-flashlight part, but not being a cop. His dad was a cop.

"Dude, it was in, like, Samuel Walton's last will and testament that travelers always be allowed to stop at Wal-Mart, no matter what. They can't go against his last wish. I mean, technically they can, they can come out and tell you to move or whatever, but when it comes down to it, ask to see Wal-Mart's bylaws. They can't make you move."

"I think the Wal-Mart guy had the right idea," John replied to our visitor. "He just didn't know how out of control it'd get."

"Yeah, he wasn't a bad guy," our visitor said.

"I think he just wanted to make stuff less expensive for people," I added. "He didn't know how badly it'd ruin small business."

"It's ruined our whole nation's economy," John said.

"What if they had just like one Wal-Mart in every state or something. Then it couldn't get too big."

I didn't know whether our visitor meant one single retail outlet location per state, or one separate superstore company in each state. Either way, I didn't think it would work.

The kids slept with John and I, up on the top bunk above the driver's seat, and the hitch-hiker slept on Sophie's bed down below. It was pretty cramped up in our bed, especially because of how much the kids rolled around. Lyric, who was sleeping at the far edge nearest the window, would often try to escape in his sleep, climbing over Sophie and me before I pushed him back into his spot. After four or fives times of being squished underneath Lyric, Sophie moved towards the foot of the bed, sleeping with her face near our feet and her feet even with my stomach, which got a few kicks. She slept like that for most of the night but turned around again and curled up next to me again about daybreak. About this time as well, I heard our visitor get up. I hoped he wouldn't leave without saying good-bye. I couldn't climb down from the bed, because John was between me and the edge. I heard the door open and shut; I smelled cigarette smoke. We had left the windows open for breeze, so he was probably smoking just outside the door. Then I didn't hear him for a while. Then he came back.

I had been lying awake for most of the night and was quite tired of it, so I finally climbed over John, waking him up but getting only a disgruntled glare in retribution. "I got to go to the bathroom," I explained as I lowered myself down from the edge of the bed.

Our friend was seated on the couch that was Lyric's bed. "I got orange juice and bagels," he told me, and I offered a thanks and a greeting. I didn't know whether the food was bought or stolen and I didn't ask. I headed into Wal-Mart to use the restroom and wash my face and curse our broken-down motorhome.

When I returned from Wal-Mart, John and the kids were sitting on the kids' beds, along with our visitor, eating bagels and drinking orange juice. I unloaded a bottle of fruit smoothie, two protein drinks, and a pound of white cheddar cheese from my purse. "I didn't know you went to work," our visitor said, and I grinned at the euphemism.

"Civil disobedience," I said. "I'm morally obligated." John took the protein drink and the cheese. "Sophie, I wish I knew where the hairbrush is. Yours needs brushed bad."

"I got one you can borrow," our visitor said. "I don't have lice or anything." He emptied out his hitch-hiker's pack, producing a small hairbrush. While I brushed Sophie's hair, he tied his sleeping bag up inside of a large handkerchief with a wolf on it. Just like a real hitch-hiker, I thought.

After we ate, we smoked another red joint while the kids ran around with a soccer ball on the asphalt. Axel came over to ask John is he wanted to go to AutoZone to check the batteries, and John agreed because then he could pick up a power steering belt while he was there. There wasn't enough room in the truck, so I intended to stay at the motorhome with the kids. But Lyric wanted to go with his dad, and then Sophie begged to go too, and I insisted I could stay at the motorhome alone.

"Are you sure?" John kept asking. "Are you sure?"

"Yeah, I'll be fine. Or are you just trying to get me to come too?" I asked, grinning.

John pressed his switchblade into my hand. It was actually *my* switchblade, but he'd misplaced his and had been carrying mine instead for a couple of weeks.

Our visitor offered to roll another joint and we went inside to do that; I deposited the switchblade on the shelf by the door. We went back outside to smoke the joint.

"Do you think that stuff about Axel is true?"

"What, like him being a Hell's Angel?"

"Yeah, that stuff. Him being wanted by the police in Colorado Springs. People don't just say stuff like that to people they've just met."

I exhaled. "Hard to tell. Doesn't matter so much to me as much as, you know, the stuff about him helping out with jobs for the homeless. I think he did that. If it was just him working, he wouldn't need so many snow shovels."

"You guys are really, like... vocal about homeless people."

"Yeah, well, it's not a lot of fun. A lot of people don't choose to live like this. And a lot of people don't feel like they have a voice, or if they do, no one listens. People only listen to us because they don't know we're homeless. We figure we should do what we can."

"Working at the gas station in town, I hated homeless people. I mean I worked third shift, so I got all the crazy tweakers, ya know? But I felt like, man, what are you doing? Ruinin' it for the rest of us. Tweakers give all the drifters a bad name. Drifters, hitch-hikers, couch-surfers, you know. 'Transients,' whatever they call us. Fuckin' tweakers, everyone thinks we're all the same. I was always like, what are you doin', ruining it for the rest of us?"

The neighbor from the camper-trailer, Billy, came out with a bowl to share, but it tasted terrible. Billy looked about thirty, and was as paunchy in his belly as Axel, but without Axel's broad shoulders and thick chest and biceps. However, Billy managed to avoid the white-and-doughy look out of sheer dirtiness.

"What is this? Spice?" our visitor asked as he exhaled a puff of dirty smoke.

"Nah, man, it's trim. We got like a pound of it for free."

I used to smoke trim when we lived in Kansas; I was growing a couple plants in the basement and when there wasn't anything in Wichita to buy, we smoked the trim. It tasted like burnt grass or maybe pond algae and gave me a headache.

"So, the wife and I are just going to take the wheels off the trailer, set it right up on cinder blocks. Build a house around it. Everything up on cinderblocks."

"What, here in the Wal-Mart parking lot?" the hitch-hiker asked. I looked at Billy's expanding puddle.

"No, we found some land and stuff, they just let you build on it."

"Where?"

"Kansas. We're gonna head there as soon as we can."

I stopped mid-hit. "You're kidding! No way! John and I just spent half our life getting out of Kansas. Why the fuck do you wanna go to Kansas?"

"Well, for one thing, the cops are better there."

"No, they're not!"

"Well, where we're going, they are. Going to a little tiny town. Only forty-two people. Everybody knows everybody."

"Better hope you like those forty-two people," the hitch-hiker said.

"Cops here suck," Bobby continued. "They hate me. Every time they arrest me, they cuff me and I'm like, really? And I do this." He held his hands behind his back for a moment, then brought them forward, wrists upturned, like an offering. The hitch-hiker glanced sideways at me. "So, the next time they come, they put two pairs of cuffs on me. And I do it again."

"Ohh, you mean you broke them?"

"Damn straight I broke 'em! I bench press six hundred pounds. And that's just for fun. Man, the cops come, and they're like, 'Billy, don't try nothin' now.' And the first cop comes and I just-- WHAM!" He continued his story while our hitch-hiker friend continued baiting him and I kept my eyes down, smoking and waiting for John and the kids to get back, and wondering if I possibly should have held on to the switch blade because Billy was having a very difficult time discerning between fantasy and reality.

Well, none of the batteries were any good-- couldn't hold a charge at all. John did get a power steering belt, though. So I took the kids to catch the city bus so we could open up the bookstore, and John waited for a guy to come fix his truck. Then he came to the shop too, and we had Open Mic Night, and we wanted to tell Dustin about our friend whose name we never knew and how he slept on our couch and was waiting for friends to give him a ride to New Mexico. But we couldn't. Because bookstore owners aren't supposed to live in broken-down motorhomes at Wal-Mart.

We never found out the kid's name. Our hitch-hiker, our visitor, whatever. John had asked him his name, but promptly forgot it. The kid did leave behind a few things: a notebook, on which he'd been breaking up weed and rolling his joints, as well as the watermelon joint paper. The notebook was mostly empty, but had a few sketches of large breasts on the first page, and a poem on the last page. I have transcribed a few decipherable lines here, in case anyone recognizes this writing or this character, so that due credit may be given:

> *Why should I explain myself*
> *I'm just like everyone else*
> *feel the need to get lost*
> (crossed out and illegible)
> *Doesn't mean with the best* (illegible)
> *leave it up to circumstance,*
> *put it all in someone else's hand*
> *just a part of the master plan*
> *& courage and action*(?) (illegible)

The day after our Open Mic Night was a city-wide event called the ArtWalk. It was supposed to be a cultural event drawing more than 50,000 tourists. We had paid $300 to be official sponsors of the ArtWalk, and to be included on their map of events. Our landlord, a terribly ineffective and disengaged woman, had paid an additional $700 to bump up our sponsorship to the next level, in exchange for her building's logo being used on the advertisements alongside our own. For her $700, we would get a live musician at each of the three ArtWalks that summer.

Our bookstore was in a window-front unit of a curious building called Old Town Marketplace. Originally the very first JC Penny building, 322 Main had also been a thrift store and a warehouse. Now, terribly outdated and negligent in its electrical work and plumbing, the building housed ten or so units on the first floor, with a large lobby in the middle. Stairs in the center of the lobby led up to a mezzanine with an additional ten units, with a walkway bordering the entire center of the mezzanine. Thus, the lobby was open to the people on the walkway above, with two rows of stores neatly stacked atop each other, and lots of open space in the middle.

When we had first opened the bookstore, we were on the second floor; Rent was cheap and it was a perfect start-up. Or so we thought. As I said to Axel, it was an inexpensive business to open; We opened our doors for business on an investment of about eight hundred dollars. We paid a deposit and rent, a whopping $400 total, and we bought business cards (I was 'Manager and Purveyor of Fine Literature'; John was 'Owner and Book Connoisseur'), and we paid $260 for the stock of a used bookstore that was closing in Fort Collins, and I think we paid anywhere from fifty to a hundred dollars for shelving; construction materials; a coffee table; and an oversized armchair. We got another couple of chairs for free from a hotel in Louisville that was being remodeled, and then we started contacting self-published authors.

This was, in my professional opinion, the genius behind our plan. We had our shelves pretty well stocked with shoddy used books, and then we got ahold of a list of self-published authors in Colorado. We told them, hi, we have a bookstore, we'd like to carry your book. And they would say SURE because no one-- Not Barnes & Noble, not the independent bookstores, not even the used bookstores-- will stock self-published books. And I don't just mean that they won't pay for self-published books; they won't waste shelf space on them, even if they can get them for free.

Well, we got ours for free. Self-published authors, many of whom has spent years on their book, were desperate to see it in a bookstore. So they'd agree to a consignment contract; We would hold the books on our shelves, and pay the authors when their books sold. We weren't taking advantage of the self-published authors or anything; Most were genuinely happy with the arrangement, and it allowed us to spend more money on other things, like holding events for our authors. Other bookstores would charge authors-- sometimes five hundred or a thousand dollars-- for a book-signing. We booked events with authors for free. And because we only carried books from authors in the state of Colorado, almost all our authors lived close enough to book an event with us. It was a perfect business model-- Apart from the fact that we failed to take into consideration that people don't buy books any more.

The location might have been a problem, too; Or, the town of Longmont's attitude towards the location. Small business was in vogue, but only *successful* small business. Whereas Boulder had an appreciation for the handmade, Longmont considered the DIY a hobby for the impoverished. And every business in Old Town Marketplace had a DIY air to it; whether it was the electrical work, the partitions and walls, the paint jobs, or the products themselves.

And I wish I didn't have to specify this, but Longmont avoided Old Town Marketplace also because of a racial bias. Of the twelve occupied shops, nine were owned by first-generation Mexican families; a Catholic bookstore, a cafe that sold only instant coffee, two fashion shops, a toy store, a snack store that sold pinatas, a shop that sold long-distance calls to Central and South America, a jewelry repair shop, and a videography and karaoke service for weddings and quiencieneras. Of the three remaining shops, one was a bike repair shop owned by a white boy with the last name Hernandez (he spoke no Spanish and once confessed to us that he felt guilty for 'fitting in' due only to his last name), one was an alterations and dress shop owned by a blond, white middle-aged woman who practiced Paganism but voted Republican, and the twelfth was us. Eight units were empty.

Longmont was about evenly divided between Latinos and white people, and when visiting the town, we had noted the Mexican restaurants and markets, the Latino art fairs and cultural events, the museums and music, and it hadn't occurred to us at all that the town was largely segregated. Oblivious, never the target of racial epithets, we assumed the town was culturally diverse and accepting, based on the sheer volume of minority businesses. It wasn't until we'd rented an apartment and our business was firmly established that we realized that we'd settled in a racially-divided clash zone.

At any rate, twice a week or so, a family of patrons would enter the Marketplace, only to say, "Oh... it's only Mexican shops..." and leave. And this is the nicest variation of what the patrons said. Spic, grease-back, dirty, and trashy were also some words used. And I am not simply inferring this from the patrons' quick exits; they said it loud enough for us to hear. Even when our shop was upstairs.

Nor did we have the business of the Latino community. I can understand their resentment; We took up space in a shop that, formerly, had been a space all their own, and we lured white customers into the run-down Old Town Marketplace, who either were patronizingly overjoyed to discover a buy-local yuppie-type bookstore in the quaint and run-down atmosphere of the former warehouse and empty units and uncovered electrical plugs and massive quantities of pinatas, or else were outright critical and disgusted with the marketplace. I can't say I blame the other shopkeepers for resenting us and our customers, but God was it frustrating. Especially once we were homeless.

Anyway, the ArtWalk was that Friday, and we anticipated that it would be a helpful event for us, both in terms of sales and exposure. We were on the ground-floor in a window-front unit then (when one of the fashion shops moved to a new location, we relocated from our upstairs unit to a larger space in a better location in Old Town Marketplace) and we figured that with all the people on Main Street, all celebrating local arts, how could we not do well?

It was a nerve-wracking day, mostly due to anticipation; First, Sophie and I went to shower at the rec center where it only costs a dollar but the shower room is a large square lined with shower heads and there is no privacy, and I fought with Sophie over washing her hair, and I scrubbed the dirt from my feet with a paper towel, and I gasped in surprise as another patron entered the locker room as I was applying lotion to my naked body, and I put on a short red sundress and tried my hardest to keep Sophie from getting dirty on the walk back to the shop. Then, John took Lyric to the showers-- and god knows what kind of trouble he had; I didn't ask. While John and Lyric were gone, one of our artists, Brian Hackworth, brought in some extra watercolor paintings and a table for the event, and sort of glared around the shop at its embarrassing emptiness.

I understood. We had been holding about two thousand dollars' worth of paintings for Brain since February, and hadn't sold one yet. Some were pricey, but a few were affordable, costing as little as fifty dollars unframed. And the prices were clearly displayed on the frames. But Brain, sensing their lack of success, had dozens of prints made on greeting cards, so that anyone could enjoy his artistic splendor for only a few dollars. These didn't sell either. Nothing much sold in our store. To the best of my knowledge, nothing much sold anywhere in the economy of 2013, except the necessities like coffee and toilet paper.

After John returned, we argued briefly over the legality of serving beer at our event, and finally I agreed that John could go get some, with the understanding that it was to be poured into paper cups, and to be served only to *friends*, not customers. I didn't even bother trying to argue about limits on his personal consumption. Whatever happened, happened. While John was gone to pick up the beer, another friend stopped by-- a rather libertarian ex-Mormon named Sam.

I had only met Sam once before, the previous day, when he had stopped by our shop during a bus layover on his way from Denver to Fort Collins for a job interview, but we had been communicating on the internet for a couple months. He was a fellow recently-emigrated inhabitant of Colorado. Sam was on his way back to Denver that Friday afternoon, and had another layover in Longmont, so he stopped by the shop again. John returned and offered Sam a beer, in a can. He had bought a mixed-case sampler from a local craft company called Ska Brewing, and their stouts and nut brown ales were alright, but I detested the yellow pilsner and lager. Then again, I detested anything light enough to see through. Even dark beer was difficult for me to stomach. I hated the bitterness. To be honest, I really don't care for alcohol at all. This has made me unpopular at parties, despite my complete willingness to inebriate myself with weed.

So Sam drank a yellow pilsner and John had something darker that I probably would have preferred and I nervously arranged refreshments on our coffee table instead of drinking anything because I didn't want to encourage it. Between a fruit tray and a vegetable tray, I placed a box of what had originally been fifty cookies, but a dozen had been eaten the night before at our Open Mic Night.

A group of about three middle-aged couples, bordering on elderly, entered the shop; They all looked somewhat the same and milled about, so I didn't get a solid count of how many people or pairs there actually were. One woman with very dark, freshly-applied port-colored lipstick asked me where Brian was.

"Oh, he should be here about six to start setting up." It was about five-forty. "The ArtWalk doesn't actually start till six-thirty but I expect he'll be back by six to set up his art."

The group inspected several books, met up with each other, parted ways again, and grazed at the refreshment table. I glared at one elderly gentlemen in particular, adorned with large tufts of hair sprouting from his ears, who planted himself in front of the table and selected all the freshest pieces of fruits, eating them directly from the tray, before moving on to the cookies.

The mauve-lipped woman approached me again. "Will you tell Brain that we came by? We have to make my granddaughter's recital so we've got to scram." She gave us a name, which I promptly forgot, then headed out the door, followed by her troupe of retirees.

Sam left soon after, and then the nervous waiting game began. Brian showed up, and we told him about his visitors (John remembered the woman's name), and Brian told us they were regulars at the cafe where he worked. With Brian standing near a display of his paintings and greeting cards, I became even more nervous. I made a pot of coffee and poured it into our carafe, and set it out on top of the antique record player we used as a second coffee table. I went to get cups, too, but we only had a few left.

"John, where are the cups you got?" I asked.

"What cups? I didn't get any cups."

"I thought that's what you were doing when you went to go get beer."

"No. I just got beer."

"Well... We only have like six cups left... How are we going to serve coffee and beer in cups without cups?"

John left to go get cups and I was left awkwardly anticipating some customers while Brian glowered from his display table. I made a show of pacing back and forth from the computer to the door, pretending to be awaiting the arrival of the musician assigned to our venue for the evening. I was more anxious for customers.

After a long wait, a white-haired and genteel old woman in a light wool dress suit entered the shop.

"Excuse me, can you show me where Gail Storey's book is?" she asked politely.

"Of course," I exclaimed, and then promptly developed a crippling case of the hiccups.

"I saw the notice about the event in the paper," she said.

"Yes, it's next-- Oh, excuse me. I'm so sorry."

"It's quite alright," the woman replied graciously. I got the impression that she was very aware of her own primness, and was self-conscious of making others feel less prim. I liked her and was horridly embarrassed.

"The event is next Friday, and Gail Storey and her husband-- I'm sorry." I hiccuped again.

"It's alright, no need," the woman insisted. "You see, Porter Storey's mother was a dear friend of mine. When I read the name in the paper, I wondered if it was the same Porter Storey, so I called her up. I would very much like to purchase the book so that I can read it before attending the event." I sold the woman the book, and my experience with her somewhat relieved my apprehension that we would have an unsuccessful evening. But she was our last customer until well after John returned.

Traffic on Main Street was blocked off so that pedestrians could have free reign of the road, and from our storefront window we could see people beginning to mill about in the street. I noticed a tall man with a bowl cut peering around the entrance to our store; I stepped out and approached him.

"Do you work here?" he asked, gesturing to our doorway.

"Yes," I replied.

"I'm Jon. I'm one of the musicians..." he trailed off.

"Oh, yes, we've been expecting you. What can I do to help you set up?"

"Ah, well, actually I think I'm going to go grab a bite to eat, then bring my equipment in. Where would you like my stuff?"

I located an area outside our store, in the lobby of Old Town Marketplace in front of our black-and-white mural of Hunter S. Thompson, where an extension cord could be thrown over one of our partitions to reach an outlet inside our shop. There were not electrical outlets in the lobby. Jon the musician left, and I returned to the shop.

"Some dancers are setting up outside," my husband John said.

"Where?" I asked.

"Right in front of our shop. Towards Third."

I took Sophie and Lyric and we headed out of the shop, south towards Third Street. A large square of blue gymnastic mats were set up in the middle of Main, and a dozen pre-teen girls in purple spandex were lounging about and chatting; a few were stretching. We stood watching them for a few minutes, and I answered the children's continuous questions as best I could. The performance finally began and we watched a mediocre number or two before I corralled the children back inside.

When we returned to the shop, about six people were wandering around, looking at books, but no one had bought anything yet. Another group was outside of the store, taking turns getting their pictures taken in front of our giant Hunter S Thompson mural, the lenses of his Aviator glasses, two feet tall, staring down at the patrons like the eyes of T J Eckleburg. At least we were starting to get some guests; hardly avoidable, as Main Street was now packed with people and they spilled into every open shop, if only because they were seemingly pushed there by the ebb and flow of the tide of people, and they stared unseeingly around them, wandering in circles and bumping into things, until by chance they found their way back into the main current of Main Street again.

Jon the musician had also returned and was setting up his amplifier and guitar in front of the Hunter S Thompson mural. He also had a banjo, and we were told by the ArtWalk representative that he was a 'traditional Irish musician,' but he was undoubtably American and seemed to play folk music of every national origin.

Sophie and Lyric danced in the lobby with a few other children while Jon the musician played the fiddle. As customers came and went, John and I stood nervously at the front of the store, informing those who asked that we 'sell independently-published books from authors here in Colorado' and that 'we never send our customers' money out of the state of Colorado.' We encouraged everyone we met to sign up for our monthly newsletter, and we sold a couple of used books and one of Brian's greeting cards, printed with his watercolor painting of a lighthouse in Santa Monica. Brian seemed to be having the same experience; he stood by his display with his girlfriend, and told superficially-curious groups about his vision of the intersection of architecture and nature. I'm sure that I would have felt differently if I were an artist, but the statement struck me as generic and vague in its profoundness. Brian's artwork, as well, was truly impressive in its quality and color, and the scenery was beautiful, as scenes of Hawaiian bungalows and Grecian vistas are meant to be.

The children started getting too wild in their dance, their flailing becoming hazardous to passer-bys, so I brought them back into the shop to take a time-out break. Not long after, Dustin and his girlfriend arrived; I should mention that in addition to being very talented and, more importantly, driven, the other reason I liked Dustin was because he bought books. He bought one used book-- *Mountain Lion Alert*, a guidebook for hikers-- and a poetry chapbook. I wondered if the Mountain Lion book was connected to his plans this fall; it was the first used book he'd ever bought from us. Mostly he bought various poetry books; not anthologies, but works by single poets. I loved him for that. On previous occasions, Dustin's dad had bought some used classics and his mother had bought my novel and a 'Buy Local Literature' t-shirt from us. The t-shirt was a gift for Dustin.

Soon after Dustin left, two women and a girl entered the shop; the girl was about six and quickly found the play table in our children's section, and John released our children to go play with her. One of the women was in her mid-twenties and had a barbell piercing through the center of her bottom lip, so that the ball rested in the dimple above chin. The other might have been fifty, or a forty-year-old smoker, and she was dressed casually but attractively, which detracted from her slightly-overweight frame. Once the young girl was playing with Sophie and Lyric, the two beaming women happily turned their attention to John and I. John gave them our thirty-second elevator speech about supporting local and independently-published authors, and the two women exchanged a glance.

John and I knew that glance; it meant that one of them either had a book or was working on a book. Once we told people that we were interested in independently- and self-published books, we often saw that look. We had begun to find that everyone was an author, or knew an author; mothers, teachers, retirees, off-duty police officers. But they never told anyone, because the general public expected authors to live that glamorous life that authors are expected to live, selling lots of books and doing signings and getting their name in the New York Times. Ashamed that they hadn't accomplished any of that, or even sold more than a handful of books, most authors kept themselves a secret.

Until they found out that we were interested in independently- and self-published books. Then there was a glance: a moment where they decided whether or not to share their secret with us. Some were nervous we wouldn't want *their* book, and that they would be again shamed for not being a *real* author. We never did that; in our opinion, if someone finished a book and published it, they met all the requirements of being a real author, New York Times be damned. Sometimes we got a book that needed a little more work-- or a lot of work-- but if it wasn't professional enough in its quality, and we couldn't risk readers getting a bad impression of independently-published books from it, then we would direct the author to other services to help them improve the quality of their book, whether an editor or a graphic designer or anything else they might need. Sometimes we even proofread for authors, if we particularly liked their story and we wanted it on their shelves but they couldn't afford a line-editor.

But we never flat-out and irrevocably turned a book down. We believed in quality literature, but we also believed that anyone could be a 'real' author with enough hard work and, yes, help. God knows the drones in the big publishing houses got all the help they needed. And they still produce the same celebrity tell-all garbage year after year.

The two women looked back at us, after their long glance

at each other had turned playful; a positive sign.

"My mother writes books," the younger woman with the piercing said.

"Really? What kind?" I said, as if I were totally shocked.

"Well... mostly I have been publishing e-books. I haven't printed any yet," the mother confessed, visibly cringing. I could tell she felt ashamed to mention e-books in a bookstore. She didn't feel like a real author.

"That's awesome!" I said. She perked up. "E-books are a great way to break into publishing. It's cheaper, and you can build up a following. What genre do you write?"

Again, she cringed. "Um... well mostly romance novels right now but I'm hoping to get into some stuff that's a little more... literary. I don't, you know, write smut or anything like that."

"Hey, you're writing," John said. "That's impressive enough. And as long as people keep reading romance, there has to be someone to write it." I was glad John handled that remark, because I wasn't quite sure how to spin it. Maybe I would have asked her about what 'literary' books she was planning on writing.

"We have a monthly newsletter that includes all of our events for the upcoming month," I added. "We have a lot of author events like book-signings, but we also have writing workshops and seminars for authors. Would you be interested?"

Both the women signed up for the newsletter, and we told the mother that if she ever got her books in print, to be sure to come by with a couple copies. She enthusiastically agreed, and she and her daughter browsed around the shop for quite a bit. Then the woman gave us a big smile and a wave before leaving with her daughter and granddaughter.

Now that Sophie and Lyric's playmate was gone, I decided to take them outside again to see what sort of festivities there were on Main Street. As I attempted to lead the children through the lobby, I overhead a conversion between a pretty, young Latina woman, and her own overweight mother.

"Well, his birthday is coming up," the elder woman said.

"I have to get him something anyway."

"Okay, but Mom, if you're going to get him something, can you at least get him a book instead of a toy?"

"Oh, he doesn't want a book. Do you, Jorge?"

They were joined by a boy of about six, who I had seen in our shop a few minutes earlier, clutching a used copy of a Three Little Pigs variation and begging his father to buy it.

"Your mother wants me to get you an old rocket science book," the grandmother said sarcastically. Her daughter flushed with embarrassment and they all left Old Town Marketplace without buying anything, even a toy.

Outside of the Used Book Emporium, half-a-block north of us, there was a face-painting booth and a long line of children, but it seemed to cost money so I prodded the children onwards, past the urns of fragrant spring flowers that lined Main Street. Under a canopy in the center of the street, an artist hawked a dozen colorful and compartmentalized oil paintings of domestic animals. Lyric and Sophie politely asked to pet the Great Pyrenees that was tethered to the artist's canopy pole. A little beyond that, still in the center of Main, a crowd engulfed a large tent lined with tables. Volunteers handed out wooden cigar boxes and all manner of craft supplies: Paint, glue, glitter, stickers, gemstones, baseball cards, foam shapes, string, ribbons, bows, fake flowers, beads, and the like. I helped the children each decorate a box with too much glue and then we took them back to the shop to show Daddy.

John was busy moving books when we returned; a so-called customer had leaned against a bookshelf, causing it to tilt its contents onto the floor. In his hurry to right it, the so-called customer knocked a display shelf loose from the wall. John was working quickly to repair the damage, re-adhering the shelf to the wall with a few quick spurts from a cordless power drill and replacing the books on the shelf, but the store had already essentially cleared out. The customer was so-called because he didn't actually buy anything. He was probably embarrassed.

Out of the businesses in our immediate vicinity-- our

bookstore, the other shop-owners, the artist, and the musician--
Jon the musician was having the most success. A large crowd had
gathered in the lobby to listen to his folk music, which actually
was Irish now, and John had found a hat in our back room and set
it out for tips; it was now overflowing. I was happy people tipped
the musician well, and he deserved it, but I failed to understand
the aversion to spending money in the store.

John and I had a quarrel over disciplining the children for
taking food from the snack trays, and John took the children back
outside in the waning dusk to see what, and how, other stores
were doing. I stayed at the shop with my ever-strained synthetic
smile, pretending that it didn't bother me that people weren't
coming in to the shop.

Brian packed up and left, and I couldn't quite tell if he was
disappointed or angry, and to be honest I'm not sure which I
would have preferred. I also could not discern whether the
emotion was in response to the current state of affairs, or at me
specifically. After he left, I resisted the urge to completely break
down into tears, which was lucky because then a friend named
Marco showed up.

Marco had been in to the shop a few times before, along
with his three-year-old daughter, Carmen. Although she was the
same age as Sophie, she seemed a little less mature than Sophie;
then again, Sophie seemed more mature than even her brother,
who was a year older. Marco's wife was also in attendance, and I
had not met her before; She and Marco were both freelance web-
designers, and previously Marco had brought Carmen to the shop
while they were out of the house so his wife could work
uninterrupted.

Our conversation was not interesting; Marco's wife and I
mainly discussed the composting of household waste using a
specific breed of earthworm, while Marco spoke with Jon the
musician, who was an old friend of his. However, the first time I
met Marco, he told me something I will never forget. Marco had
been in Nicaragua after college, 'for the revolution,' he said, and
he had translated a book of Nicaraguan poetry. Marco had told me

about a 'culture of poetry' in Nicaragua that was vital both to the culture and the politics of the region, and that-- this is what I will never forget-- the national Nicaraguan newspaper had a Poetry section, like how national American newspapers have Business and Sports News sections.

I'm still waiting for a Poetry section in our paper.

Carmen began to get upset with her stroller, and Marco and his wife thought it best to leave, and I knew the kids would be sad to have missed one of their few peers. I set about cleaning up after the event; or, I picked up a few wadded-up napkins from near the fruit tray, then sank into the couch in exhaustion and disappointment.

"Nobody's selling anything," John announced as he and the children entered the shop half-an-hour later. "We went around to tons of different galleries, and nobody's buying any art. Everybody's just here to *pretend* they support art."

"Well, then I suppose Brian can't be too mad that he didn't sell anything here, if none of the artists are selling anything anywhere," I replied.

"I didn't say no one had bought anything at all," John said. "But no one's buying art. No one came here to buy it. They just came here to *pretend* to support art. You can't pretend to support art unless you support that artist and you have to spend *money* to support the artist. Facebook likes don't fucking pay the rent."

I nodded sympathetically and the children helped themselves to the grapes in the fruit tray.

"I started that book," I told John. I meant This Book.

"Oh?" he asked. "I thought you weren't going to."

"I changed my mind. I decided to after all."

"Why'd you change your mind?" John asked.

"After our conversation with Dustin last night. I wanted so badly to tell him about everyone we've met. And I wanted to warn him. And I couldn't."

"You don't think he should do it?"

I hesitated. "I think he should if he wants to. But he doesn't know how hard it will be. Kerouac made it look like fun."

"Kerouac also had a steady supply of money, whether from his family or the G.I. Bill or whatever. You know? He never had to live like this if he didn't want to."

"Exactly," I said. "He could quit or take a break if he wanted to. We can't just quit being homeless. We don't have the money to have options."

"We did when we started," John said, and I realized with a jolt that he was right. "We stayed in hotels and stuff whenever we needed a shower. We were spoiled like Kerouac. We kinda had an endless supply of money to do whatever we wanted."

But it wasn't endless. It had run out.

Two

The money had run out in December. We had moved out here in September, after a month of camping wherever we pleased. I had laser aberration surgery for an immunodeficiency-related cervical cancer, which sounds very sci-fi and futuristic, at the Wichita Surgery Center on September eighteenth, the date our lease ended at our duplex in Wichita. We stayed in a hotel that night while I recovered in a daze of hyrdocodone, and the next day we left the hotel and drove west with all of our belongings in a U-Haul trailer hauled by John's truck. Packing all of our belongings while I prepared for surgery was one of the hardest things I have ever done.

In October we had opened the business, and it was small but it was going well. Authors and publishers around Colorado started getting excited about us. I was in remission from both cancer and lupus. We still had plenty of operating capital. And then we got a letter from my insurance company, and they weren't going to pay for laser aberration, and I should have known that the cocktail of toxic hydroxychloroquine and immuno-suppressants would give me cancer. In November, I paid my hospital bills. And in December, we ran out of money.

I don't mean we were low on money. We had zero point zero zero dollars in our bank account.

Still, we showed up to work every day, even though no customers did. We might go a week without a serious browser, let alone a purchase. On Mondays we went to the food pantry and got as much stale bread as we could carry. We applied for food stamps. We applied for as many jobs as we could. We scoured

Craigslist for gigs, and John and his truck helped a lot of people move. I sold every ounce of silver or gold that I had inherited from dead grandmothers. We burned wood for heat instead of using gas or electricity.

In January we got an eviction notice while waiting for my student loans to be transferred to our bank account. I was taking classes, still, at Wichita State University; they were all online classes and I took them remotely. I was still enrolled under a pre-law scholarship that covered my tuition, but in our dire circumstances, I decided to take out the loan available to me.

We paid rent and avoided eviction by less than forty-eight hours. We paid some more hospital bills. We bought Lyric a used mattress, donated his toddler bed, and bought him a new duvet emblazoned with Batman. We purchased some stock for the bookstore from more well-known independent authors and publishers who could afford to turn down a consignment contract.

We did alright in February. We signed a lease addendum to move from the isolated upstairs unit in Old Town Marketplace to the more attractive-- and visible-- window-front unit. We found graffiti and mural artists willing to embellish our walls for a book-trade. We opened shop again in our new location, with Hunter S Thompson on the outside wall and someone's graffitied laughing child and the Colorado state flag behind the children's section and a couch, respectively. But we didn't make enough sales. And we didn't make enough money. And we couldn't make March's rent.

The day before we were evicted was the day of Central Elementary's craft fair. The school was holding the fair on a Saturday to raise money to benefit their sister school in Uganda, and one of our clients, Jason Gage-- an illustrator, rather than an author-- had purchased a booth for the fair. But he found himself over-committed, having also signed up to play the didgeridoo at a lunch-time performance at the craft fair, and his sister unexpectedly came to visit, so Jason bequeathed his booth to us, and we took him up on the offer.

I set up our booth at the assigned table in a hallway near

the principal's office, next to a mother selling a variety of felt-bird mobiles hanging from a hand-welded frame, and across from a teacher and her six-year-old son selling knitted scarves. John and the kids helped me to carry in stock, and then they left to go seek assistance.

I arranged our newsletter sign-up sheets and stickers adorned with our logo and flyers promoting upcoming events, along with dozens of books I had selected to bring for the fair. To be fair, people did buy books; mostly the children's book that Jason Gage had illustrated, as the children recognized the name of their art teacher, but other books as well. I wrote out receipts and entered credit card numbers and reloaded our bank account webpage-- over and over and over again-- waiting for our tax return to show up. The tax refund should have been for over six thousand dollars, due in part to my excessive medical bills the previous year. The tax return should have been deposited into our bank account on February twenty-eighth, but on March sixteenth it still hadn't arrived. We had just gotten the eviction notice the evening before, upon returning from work after nine o'clock that Friday night, and the tax return was our last hope. We knew our rent was late, and the previous week, I had emailed our property manager a copy of our tax return and its expected deposit date, begging for a little more time, begging for no eviction while we waited on our tax return. I got no reply. So I suppose we were expecting the eviction, but we weren't expecting to have less than forty-eight hours' notice. We weren't expecting it to be over the weekend while nobody's office was open.

Still we kept waiting on the tax return, even as the hours disappeared before us and our eviction time crawled closer. But there wasn't much hope that our bank account would be updated on a Saturday. There wasn't much hope that anyone's office would be open on a Saturday; but still, John drove with the kids from county building to non-profit organization to payday loan shop, looking for any way to keep us in our apartment. Everywhere was closed.

At the crowded craft fair, I gave my elevator-speech about

carrying books from local, independent authors and never sending our customers' money to the Big Six publishers in New York; I expected the same polite feigned enthusiasm I received from browsers at the bookstore, and I got plenty of it, but I also sold book after book, more than we had ever sold in a single day before. More than we had ever sold in a single week. I watched the stack of receipts stack out, eagerly totaling the sales. We owed a thousand dollars in rent, but even if we paid it, we would still be required to pay three-hundred dollars in court fees to reverse the eviction.

I totaled the sales receipts: Fifty-three ninety. A hundred and twelve thirty-six. A hundred and fifty-two sixteen. Three hundred and forty-eight.

As the craft fair neared to its close, I gave up hope that we would make it. To have sold more books at one time than we had ever sold before, and yet to still be so far from making rent, was humiliating.

After the fair had ended, I sat on the stoop outside a side-door of the elementary school, clutching a box of promotional materials and leftover stock, crying for an hour before John picked me up, children in tow. The truck bed was full of liquor-store boxes, meant for our inevitable move; although to his credit, John had bought only a single forty-ounce of beer.

John took the children and me home, and he unloaded all of the empty boxes for me, filling our back porch and living room. Then he left to go back to open the shop, in an impressive display of optimism, while I was to pack our belongings. He had already packed all of our books and DVDs into liquor-store boxes and had taken them to our shop to store in our back room. The empty bookshelves stared down at me.

I didn't know what to do with the children, because it was their nap time but I needed to be able to pack their clothes from their closet, so I put the miniature VHS player in their room, and put on an old movie, and told them that they didn't have to go to sleep but they needed to stay in bed.

While desperately searching the internet for some resource

that would allow us to stay in our apartment, I had come across a checklist meant for those packing for "potential homelessness." The list was divided into time frames:

What to do if you may become homeless in the next couple months.
What to do if you may become homeless in the next two weeks.
What to do if you may become homeless in the next couple of days.
What to do if you may become homeless in a few hours.
What to do if you recently and unexpectedly became homeless.

I had skimmed the 'next couple days' section, desperate for a resource I hadn't heard of yet. Rent relief, homelessness prevention, family togetherness; all offices were closed for the weekend. But still I had culled some information: Keep all the birth certificates together in one backpack. Keep the toothbrushes here, too. Find a friend who might let you store the possessions you won't be able to carry with you. If you have any favors to call in, or anyone who will lend you money, try to borrow as much as you can because you need it now. Keep it all somewhere safe, like in a bank. Withdraw about fifty dollars to keep with you somewhere safe, like in your shoe.

I wondered what you were supposed to do if fifty dollars was all you had.

We didn't have any friends or any favors to call in, so I started packing backpacks. I went through our file folders, taking the ones we might need; taxes, birth certificates, immunization records, health insurance. Everyone's tooth brushes went in my backpack, too.

I packed the children's backpacks, which were fairly small. The plan was to pack everything that couldn't fit in the backpacks into trash bags and liquor store boxes, and take them to a storage unit; the only problem was finding a storage unit open on a weekend. Since we didn't know if it would happen, I didn't plan on us being able to pack the extra clothes, and I packed everything of importance into the backpacks; A t-shirt from Sophie's first dance recital, with her name on the back along with the forty other performers. A dinosaur t-shirt I had bought Lyric at a museum. A fair balance of long-sleeve and short-sleeve shirts; I didn't know what the remainder of March or April would bring. Every pair of long pants the children owned, which was not many, and a pair or two of shorts. And lots of socks and underwear. This was all that fit into their backpacks and it wasn't enough. Then I started packing everything else into trash bags.

"What are you doing?" Sophie asked, and I pretended I didn't hear her the first time, but it was unavoidable when I returned to their closet with a second trash bag. The kids were watching Disney's *Hunchback of Notre Dame*.

"Well, sweetie, we might be moving soon, so I'm packing up our stuff just in case." I still had hope that we'd somehow, some way, come up with the money before two-thirty the next day.

"I want to stay here," Sophie whined.

"I know, sweetie, but these apartments aren't very good for us, so we're going to try to find better ones," I told her. How do you put a positive spin on being homeless for your three-year-old child?

When John came home, I had already packed most of our clothes and was working on the dishes, moving them from cupboard to box in an automated, unstopping motion. I was so scared of running out of time. The children were happy to see John and told him gleefully about getting to watch a movie instead of taking a nap. John tore me from my mechanical, emotionless motions, squeezing my arms against my body in a tight hug, halting my work. I breathed against his warm chest, savoring his scent and the layer of cotton against my face. It's the only place I've ever felt really safe.

Words would be wasted on me, unlike his embrace, so John didn't say anything. He just held me for a few minutes before moving on to the children.

"Alright, guys, I got all these boxes here." Our living room was strewn haphazardly with dozens of boxes. "I think we should make a castle or something. What do you guys think?"

The children helped John clear out a space in the living room, pushing all the boxes against the walls, and then they built the perimeter. They stacked Svedka and Bud Light and Grey Goose boxes to make walls taller than themselves. I worried that there was something sinister in the irony; how would they remember this frolic if we ever wound up inside of a cardboard box. I supposed that homeless people didn't actually live inside boxes, but then again, I really didn't know.

They built a castle tall enough for Daddy to sit inside with them, and they built a roof from flattened boxes, and turrets and towers to scrape our low ceiling. The children played inside their castle for a long time, and then John brought out a ball.

The kids had never been allowed to play ball in the house; we had a security deposit to worry about. But now we weren't getting it back anyway, and John launched Lyric's child-sized basketball ball at the cardboard castle, knocking out a turret.

"Our castle!" Sophie and Lyric cried, and John handed them the ball.

The children's mild disappointment quickly dissipated when they realized that they would be allowed to play, too. I only watched. John devised a catapult from a stretchy exercise band, and all three took turns launching the ball at the castle until it was flattened. Then John and I put the children to bed and our work began.

I helped John carry out our antique Motorola record player, and we loaded it into the truck for John to take to the shop; the record player now functions as our coffee table, as I have mentioned. We loaded a few other things to take the shop that we couldn't carry and didn't want to leave behind, mostly furniture: an office chair, a filing cabinet, an antique or antique-looking bookshelf.

While John was gone, unloading furniture at the shop, I

finished packing the things in the kitchen: Dishes, appliances, and the contents of our spice cabinet.

When he returned, I had dumped out an old trunk full of Christmas decorations on our bedroom floor; We had thrown out all of our Christmas decorations when we left Wichita, but had inherited this trunk from the woman next door when she moved. Tacky cotton-ball Santa Claus crafts littered the floor, and I filled the trunk with things I didn't want to leave behind: My collection of antique cameras, some dresses my grandmother had sewn, a Raggedy Ann doll she had made as well. My high school diploma; although I doubted I'd ever need it to prove my graduation, I figured better safe than sorry.

John and I went to sleep, curled up together on our mattress, with an alarm set for early morning.

When we awoke, we took a long shower and made love, uncertain of when the opportunity to do either might again arise. While the children were still sleeping, we packed John's truck bed with the trunk full of things I couldn't stand to lose and the liquor-store boxes of dishes and the trash-bags of clothing, and John left for the only storage unit in town that was open on Sundays. I boiled all the eggs in our fridge in one pot we had left out, and gave the children cereal with the end of the milk, and yogurt because it wouldn't keep either. I dug boxes out of closets, like the box of bug spray and sunscreen and water floaties we only used in summer months. Another box with a table-top charcoal grill, half-a-bag of charcoal, and grill tongs and spatulas. All our sleeping bags. Our mildewy tent. The kids' box of dress-up clothing. A box of cleaning supplies. I stacked them up in the living room for when John returned.

I told the kids to each pick out three toys, and I put them in a shoe box. Sophie picked a Batman action-figure, a Rapunzel barbie doll she'd gotten for Christmas, and a Sleeping Beauty of the same type as Rapunzel, but whom she'd gotten from a garage sale instead. Cat Woman went back into the plastic toy dresser after much deliberation. Lyric picked three action figures from a Jurassic Park set that had belonged to John when he was young. I wrapped the plastic toy dresser up with tape, so that the drawers would stay shut. It went into the living room, too, to wait for John.

I filled a liquor-store champagne box with bubble bath, shampoo, the extra brand-new toothbrushes we kept under the sink to replace the children's tooth brushes just in case they got strep throat or the flu. I packed extra soap, unopened toothpaste, lotions and body sprays. I filled a trash bag with towels and bedsheets. I folded up the children's blankets, Lyric's Batman duvet and Sophie's pink one with princesses. I stacked them up on the couch with their pillows. John returned from the storage unit with an empty truck bed and a storage-unit key and plenty of complaints about hidden costs and required insurance. I helped him carry out the mattresses, the boxes, the children's toy dresser. I cried a little more and he hugged me and he left. It was noon and I gave the children hard-boiled eggs and whatever cheese we had left, along with the end of the fresh apples.

I started packing the things we would need with us, which would not go to the storage unit, and I placed them on the couch with the all our blankets: The backpacks with our clothing, the birth certificates and toothbrushes. A shopping bag with Rigby's food and water bowls, and the rest of her bag of dog food. The laptop computer, still open so that I could continue to reload our bank account page, still waiting for the IRS to rescue us.

John was still out, and we had an hour and a half before the sheriff was scheduled to come, so I cleaned out our cooler and emptied the contents of our fridge, along with the rest of the boiled eggs. I packed the nonperishable food into shopping bags, along with a can opener. Crackers and peanuts. Breakfast cereal. Fruit snacks.

John still had not returned and I was getting nervous. And then I got angry. The property managers had the nerve to kick us out with so little notice, on a weekend when they knew no resources would be available. They hadn't returned my email. They hadn't even faced us to give us the notice. They posted it on our door, while we were at work, when they knew we wouldn't see it until after their office was shut for the weekend. They had wiped their hands of us. I wanted to make them feel ashamed.

I climbed up on the couch, balancing on top of the folded duvets, and I scrawled a message in Sharpie on the wall:
"3.5 million homeless Americans.
1.6 million are children.
Today, my children are 2 more.
Thanks."

It was juvenile and rude, but then again, so was refusing to look at my face or return my messages while putting my children out on the street.

John returned, and he looked at my message on the wall, but he didn't say anything. Instead, he loaded the blankets and cooler into the truck. The kids and the dog got in, too. It was just after two o'clock, and the sheriff was scheduled to evict us at two-thirty, and we didn't want to chance meeting him. We didn't want our children to hear the police tell us to leave. We'd rather them think we were leaving willingly.

John came back inside after the kids were in the truck, and he picked up our hall closet door-- which wasn't attached to the frame, and had never been repaired no matter how many times we contacted the maintenance department-- and threw it down to the ground in our narrow hallway. He balanced on it, then bounced up and down until the wood cracked. We weren't getting our security deposit back anyway.

We left the front door unlocked and pulled out of the apartment parking lot, then stopped on the side of the road in a little slice of suburbia that was no longer ours while we deliberated where to go next. We decided on a motel in town where we knew a lot of homeless people lived. It had thirty or so units in a U-shape, with an RV park in the middle, and the office at the top of the U, which faced Main Street. It had been in business for eighty years and we assumed that at one time, it had been a camping spot and motel on the outskirts of town, but now

it was surrounded by gas stations and urban squalor. We knew
homeless people lived there because a few months before, a
Longmont police officer was honored for redirecting a homeless
man and his middle-school daughter to that RV park instead of
ticketing them for parking illegally at the fair grounds.

We inquired about vacancies at the motel, but they were
full and cost two hundred dollars a week anyway. We weren't
quite sure what to do next so we went to a park so the children
could play awhile. I wore a big brown-and-pink striped baja
hoodie that enveloped me like a shell and came to my knees, but I
started to get chilly as the sun set. I had also been too nervous to
eat lunch, so I was getting hungry as well.

"You've been homeless for two hours and you're already
cold and hungry," John remarked. "This does not bode well."

We ate hard-boiled eggs in the truck, rolling them on the
outside of the door through the open window to break the shell.
Rigby ate hard-boiled eggs too.

It was getting dark, so we headed to our shop. No other
shops in our building were open on Sundays, so we had the empty
building to ourselves. The lights in the window-front shops,
including ours, stayed on all night unless you turned off the
breaker, so we thought it best to leave them on. This meant that
anyone on Main Street could see into our shop, and the back room
was full of our belongings and was only about fifteen square feet
anyway, so I turned the couch and set up our chalkboard and
other furniture to block one corner in the back of the bookstore
from the view of late-night pedestrians that might pass by on the
Main Street sidewalk. We spread out the children's blankets in
that corner, and we slept there, side-by-side on the hard ground.

In the morning we ate breakfast at the homeless shelter
and packed our pockets with extra donuts and expired yogurt and
sausage patties wrapped in napkins, and then we went to one of
the many offices that had been closed over the weekend. They
helped us to apply for lottery-based housing assistance, and we
turned in all of our verification forms after a hectic day of
photocopying, but then the county office was notified that due to

the American Budget Sequester that took effect on March 1ˢᵗ, certain county funds were eliminated, and lottery-based housing assistance was indefinitely postponed. We spent our days trying to find food and fresh water and a shower while we ran our shop, alternating between sneaking into campgrounds late at night, sleeping at the shop, and buying a night at a motel when we could afford it, unaware until mid-April that our names would never be drawn because the lottery would never take place.

Three

We were all a little disheartened after our relative lack of success during ArtWalk that Friday in May, so before returning home to our RV in the Wal-Mart parking lot, John and I ate a bag of shrooms. John's sister had given them to us when she visited in February, and it was about four grams so it was only worth about twenty dollars on the street and it didn't seem worth the effort to find a buyer that wouldn't rat us out, so we had just been saving them. Not for a rainy day, exactly, because a rainy day seems like a terrible time to do shrooms, but for a special occasion. I guess that evening seemed as good of a time as any, to John, anyway. He ate half the bag and once it was done, I didn't want to have to sit around babysitting without tripping myself, so I ate the rest.

When we arrived at the RV, there was an unmistakable stench of urine from the puddle between our motorhome and Billy's camper, so we shut the windows and put the children to bed. This was before we started tripping, and then John decided it was as good of a time as any to watch *Who Framed Roger Rabbit?* So he took off with the laptop to the Super 8 motel across Highway 66 from the Wal-Mart, because they had wifi that was free, if you had the password. The password was the phone number of the motel, which we had known at one point because we had stayed at that motel several times before we acquired the motorhome at the end of April, but we no longer had the phone number in our possession. I suppose John left to try to surreptitiously obtain the phone number from an unsuspecting desk receptionist so he could download the movie, and I stayed in the top bunk of our motorhome, wrapped up in our duvet to protect myself from the intensity of the world around me; everything kept moving, even the walls. I have no idea how John managed to communicate with the employees of the Super 8, obtain their phone number, work the computer, and find his way back home, but I imagine it was quite the adventure. He tells me that he was talking aloud to himself for much of it.

We watched *Who Framed Roger Rabbit?* and I spent most of it either hiding in the covers again, repeating over and over that I 'couldn't handle it,' referring to the antics of the cartoon world, or laughing until I was afraid I would vomit, or crying inconsolably. Partly I was crying because we were homeless and I was afraid we would never stop being homeless; that it wouldn't be just a two-month blip on the radar of my children's childhood memories, nestled in the family photo albums somewhere between Sophie's third birthday and Lyric's fifth, but an ongoing way of life, something they would be forced to live with until they could break out of it, like hamsters from a cage. And even if they ever broke out, they might be so domesticated to life lived homeless, so adapted to the nuances of living like dirt beneath society's shoes, that they wouldn't know how to live on their own, outside the cage of poverty. Partly I was crying because the cartoons were so scary.

John and I spent most of Saturday recovering from our trip with Gatorade and cheese, which I stole from Wal-Mart, and then he went to work at the liquor store at four and I was left to run the shop and watch the children for the evening, while cleaning and preparing for another book-signing the next day. Sunday book-signings were usually less well-attended but more quiet, due to the absence of screaming children in the Old Town Marketplace lobby.

Book-signings were, as a general rule, a nerve-wracking experience, especially if no one showed up. Usually, no one did. Just the previous week, a sociologist had came to sign copies of her book, a resource guide for the family of transgender individuals. We set out a vegetable tray and cookies and miniature strawberry shortcake cupcakes-- the latter came from a food pantry bag, but they were so beautifully decorated and not quite stale yet so I set them out anyway. The author had brought bookmarks and postcards with information about her book, and a sign-up sheet for those interested in a newsletter from an organization called SOFFA, which stood for Significant Others, Family, Friends, and Allies. She also had buttons, declaring the wearer a SOFFA, and we each donned a button. John still wears his on his backpack. The author and John and I sat around the refreshment table and enjoyed lovely conversation for two hours, but nobody came. The author decided to leave, but to our relief she chalked up the zero attendees to the sensitive subject; Prospective attendees were probably scared of outing themselves, she thought. She was happy with us just for holding the event, given the subject matter, and making it known that we were supporters of transgender equality. She decided to leave her promotional materials at our shop for the week, hoping that someone would find the information helpful. She had stopped by to pick her materials up again the morning of the ArtWalk; I don't know if any buttons or bookmarks were missing, but nobody had signed up for her newsletter. Our failure to attract customers was hard on John and I, but I think the hardest part was disappointing our authors.

This Sunday, our expected author was Marianne Mitchell, a historical-fiction Young Adult author. Now in her sixties, she spent most of her adult life in the traditional publishing industry, writing children's books. This was back in the eighties, when it was possible for a human being to make a living that way. She also wrote stories for the children's magazine *Highlights*. She still does, sometimes. But you can't make a living on it any more.

She had self-published *A Promise Made* and had a few more upcoming Young Adult books that would be published through the same press. When you self-publish a book, you must create your own publishing company, which is simple and not very expensive. Hers was called Rafter Five Press, and it had a little more credibility than most; it had upcoming books from multiple authors. Her husband had been searching for a publisher for his book, and when he found none, his wife said, "I know a press that will take it."

John and Marianne and I sat around the lounge area of the bookstore, this time without any refreshments except for coffee because we were low on cash, while Marianne told us all of this.

"It's just ridiculous," she said. "I spent almost a decade sending out queries and submissions, trying to get this book published, and you know what the really disheartening part is?"

"No one replies," I said. I knew because I had done the same thing for almost seven years before giving up on traditional publishers and self-publishing my first book.

"No one even sends a reply," Marianne echoed. "You follow all of their submission guidelines, jump through all of their little hoops, and they don't even bother to dignify you with a reply. And that's not just the publishers, either. The literary agents are the worst."

John uttered his agreements about impoliteness among professionals of the industry, and I found myself thinking: She's a published author. She had successful children's books in the eighties before the publishing industry tanked. She has an ongoing column in a national magazine. She has a *name*. If she can't even get a reply from a literary agent, then how can any one *new* expect to ever get published?

"I had a dream last night," Marianne continued, and I realized that she and John had continued discussing the changing values of our society, "And I dreamed that I went back to my old Alma Mater, where I went to college. I had majored in Spanish, so I was in the Modern Languages department. And I walked into the Modern Language department, and it was totally different; Lavish awards and framed photographs on the walls of the hallways. I walked into my old Spanish seminar room, and it was no longer an auditorium, but a dance hall. Women were dancing the flamenco, and a group of people were all speaking Spanish together, and there was a buffet table at the back of the room. It was so weird that I left.

"I went into the next room, and it was the Japanese class. It was like an auditorium still, but changed; it was a giant movie theatre, with plush seats and surround-sound, and the class was watching a Japanese film projected on the wall. I left and walked into the next classroom. It was an industrial kitchen, and a cooking lesson was being given-- In Italian or French, I couldn't tell. Everyone was making pastries and elaborate dishes and it smelled so good.

"Finally, I found my old Spanish teacher, and I asked her, 'What happened?' And she told me there had been a mix-up in the budgets. 'Well, what do you mean?' I asked. 'We got the football team's budget by mistake, and they got ours.' I asked her what that meant, and she said, 'Here, let me show you,' and she took me out to the football field, and inside the field house there was a classroom, and all the great big hulky football players were crammed into these little desks, you know? The kind they had at high schools where the desk is attached to the chair, and these big guys are just crammed in, all bent down over their desks. And they're sitting there, repeating over and over again, 'I tackle, you tackle, he she and it tackles.'"

John and I burst into polite laughter at the punchline. I knew there had to be authors who memorized their stories like that. We listened politely and asked detailed questions while Marianne told us all about the town of Silver Plume, Colorado, where her book takes place, because she decided to go ahead and give her presentation to us because "no one was coming." Neither John nor I responded to that point, choosing instead to express our enthusiasm for her presentation. After a while, another of our authors showed up; he had bought Marianne's book a few weeks prior, and though he hadn't finished it yet, I was grateful he had attended the event and brought along his copy of the book for Marianne to sign. I was grateful he had bought a book to begin with it. Not many of the authors, even, bought books.

After the event, John found an ad while surfing Craigslist:

"FREE BOOKS. Self-published. Paperback. Could be taken apart to use for craft projects, or for kindling."

The ad made me very sad. It could be a story in itself-- only a little more cumbersome that Hemingway's famous Shortest Story Ever. The trials and tribulations of a lifetime were contained in that one ad.

John decided to call and ask about the books; It turned out to be a lawyer from Boulder who had self-published a novel and spent a lot of money on a lot of copies, but then hadn't had time to market them.

"It's called *The Physics of Caribou Creek*," John said.

"Cool," I said. It was the type of name I wished I had come up with.

"The worst part is that one of the Big Six were interested in it. No, I don't know which one. But they weren't going to publish it unless he took out some of the 'spiritual stuff,' whatever that means. Doesn't that suck?"

"God. Seriously? Wow. I can't believe the shit they get away with."

"I know, right? Everything's trimmed and tailored to fit the mainstream. Not an ounce of diversity. It's sick how they'll give best-selling publishing packages for a celebrity tell-all but can't risk anything on a new story from a new author."

"New authors might now sell. New stories might not sell," I said, looking around the empty store.

"So, anyway," John went on, opting to ignore my self-deprecating jab at our store. "He decided to self-publish so he could keep the story as he wanted to tell it. I don't know who the fuck he went through, but it sure wasn't no print-on-demand site. He wound up with, like, a garage full of boxes of books but no one to sell them to. He works as a lawyer so he didn't have time for marketing. And you have to be your own marketing company to move any amount of self-published books, but a whole garage full?"

"Jeez," I said. "So he's just going to give them to us for free?"

"That's what he said. We just have to go pick them up in Boulder."

"Well, looks like we're going to Boulder," I said. So we did, that evening.

We dropped off three boxes of forty-two copies of *The Physics of Caribou Creek* at the shop, then went home to sleep for a while. John and Lyric left the motorhome early Monday morning to catch a shuttle bus from Wal-Mart to the Denver International Airport, and to fly from there to Kansas City where John's aunt lived. Then she drove John and Lyric to Wichita in time for John's sister's graduation late Monday afternoon. It was the first time John had seen much of his family since before Lyric was born, and the first time I was away from John for longer than a day since we moved to Colorado. Mondays are our day off at the bookstore-- the one day of the week we're closed-- but Sophie and I went anyway, so I could use the internet and so she could make crafts out of glitter-glue, which was a project I was hesitant to do with Lyric. I printed off an application for food stamps, after being told Friday that my previous application had expired and I needed to re-apply, and then Sophie and Rigby and I walked to the Housing and Human Services building and dropped off the application, and then we went to the park so Sophie and Rigby could run around. But it started raining, so I put Rigby in the truck and took Sophie to the library instead.

Monday night I dreamed that John got home late at night after hitch-hiking from Wichita, and he got into bed next to me and I fell asleep in his arms and when I woke up alone I was very disappointed.

Tuesday morning I began eagerly anticipating John's return, partly because of the previous night's dream and partly because I had no idea when he would be home but I hoped it would be before the event that night. We had been planning the event with Lawrence Gladeview for months. He was one of my favorite poets, after Dustin. I hoped John would make it home that evening; his mother had bought John and Lyric a one-way

plane ticket to Kansas, and had insisted she would drive him back
to Longmont, but John didn't want her to because he didn't want
her to know we were homeless. Also he wasn't even sure she'd do
it. So instead, John had been trying to find a ride-share on
Craigslist, and told me that if he couldn't find one, he would
hitch-hike. Like the great Kerouac, right? I was scared for that.

Sophie and I stopped at Target before work, and I returned
a pair of flip-flops my mother had mailed me for my birthday.
The customer service representative gave me about seventeen
dollars back on a gift card, and I bought refreshments and napkins
for the event. I also shoplifted a new dress for myself, wanting to
look sophisticated, and a new dress for Sophie too.

I spent the morning nervously cleaning the shop;
arranging craft supplies and napkins and paper cups on the
shelves behind the counter, sweeping up crumbs, wiping down
the coffee tables and wooden chairs. I was rearranging a display
shelf to include books by the poets that would be featured at the
event that night when the phone rang.

"Hello, we're giving you a call back about the services you
have applied for last week." I had gotten probably a dozen calls in
the past two months that had began that way, and had applied for
services with at least a dozen more organizations that never called
back. I asked her which organization she was with, and she told
me the Tree House.

"Ohh, you're the homeless shelter in... um... Wheat Ridge,
right?"

"Yes, that is correct. What I'm going to do now is ask you
some questions for our screening, and then next week you need to
call us back and ask to have an intake form completed. Once we
complete your intake form, it will be about three to eighteen
months before we are able to place you."

"Okay, great," I said. Eighteen months only sounds great
if you've applied for as many full shelters as I have, been put on
as many waiting lists, been told it will be years before space
opens up.

I gave her my social security number, and those of John

and the children, and answered questions about our employment.

"And where are you staying right now?" the technician asked, and right then, a man I didn't recognize walked through the door, along with Lawrence Gladeview.

"Can I... can I call you back later, actually?" I asked.

"That's really all the questions I have right now. I'll process your screening and you should call back next week to ask about the intake evaluation."

She hung up and I turned my attention to Lawrence and his friend. The stranger seemed very short, but I wasn't sure if that was only because Lawrence was so tall-- well over six feet, with dark hair and a nose that I think is described as aquiline; at least, I have heard that term used to describe the noses of people whom I think look like Lawrence. His friend was shorter and rounder, and had red hair and a long red beard.

"This is John Dorsey," Lawrence said to me when I was off the phone.

"So good to meet you," I replied, shaking his hand. I recognized his name as one of the poets who would be featured at the event that night. The event was billed as a poetry tour, similar to a rock band going on tour, only it was a group of poets and they were touring bookstores in the Boulder area. Lawrence was the only one whom I had met, but if he vouched for the other poets then they were gold in my book. So was the tour. I loved everything about the concept-- I loved the idea of making poetry as accessible and desirable as music, and by extension, by making the unknown and independently-published poets as popular and sought-out as the unknown and independent-record bands that teenagers and twenty-somethings flocked to and name-dropped and collected in their repertoire. Along with visions of a Poetry section in our newspaper, I dreamed of a day when the desirable 16-to-35 crowd would brag about *discovering* an independent poet or author, they way they bragged about *discovering* an indie band.

"We just stopped by so I could show John the place," Lawrence said, waving an arm at the graffiti that decorated the wall behind the children's toy table.

"Is that the same artist who did the Hunter S. Thompson outside?" John Dorsey asked. He meant the mural on our outside wall in the lobby.

"No, actually, that one was done by a motorcycle painter from Commerce City. It's air-bushed. This one is a really talented kid from Aurora. He goes by El Netas. He was just going from business to business in Denver, looking for businesses that would let him tag their walls. He was having a hard time finding legal work, ya know? We were really excited to get him up here."

"So, he did all that with spray paint, then?" John Dorsey asked.

"Yeah, isn't that incredible? Even the tongue. It's so photorealistic, isn't it? It's also sort of impressionistic. You get real close and the tongue looks like it's just blobs of pink and white, then you stand back and it looks so real that it looks wet."

"Is it one of your kids?" Lawrence asked.

"Nah, it was just one of his friends' kids. It was incredible to watch. He just had this photograph, and he painted that from the picture, just like that. It was incredible. And then he added in all that other stuff, the cartoon-y collar and the lines."

"It's pretty cool," John said.

"I love the combination of photorealism with the more traditional graffiti-style cartoon-y stuff. It looks like he did it in Photoshop."

The men made some politely impressed noises and then looked around the shop for a bit, and then I informed Lawrence of what refreshments we would be having at the event later, and he and John Dorsey left to go rest before the event. It was almost two o'clock, so I quickly made a sign-- "Be back by three; Poetry Tour tonight; Stop back at six for poetry, wit, food, and fun!"-- and Sophie and I rushed to make it to our appointment at the Our Center.

It was the same center where we ate hot meals, where we picked up stale bread and expired yogurt from the food pantry, where the hardcore-homeless sat in the Warming Center during snowy days. As we passed the food pantry entrance, a homeless man called John Redfeather was leaving. He was not all quite there, but was very kind and said "Peace!" to everyone he met, holding up two fingers. He had taught our children how to do this, too. When Sophie saw him, she held up her fingers in the old hippie symbol and shouted "Peace! Peace!" at John Redfeather. He grinned toothlessly at her greeting and dug around in his food pantry bag until he found an apple-flavored granola bar, and offered it to Sophie. She was elated. We left John Redfeather and headed around the building to the Intake Center entrance.

Every homeless shelter in Longmont required a screening at this location; We thought we had applied for all of them, along with the lottery-based housing assistance, the first Monday we had been homeless, two months prior. But when I had been denied for food stamps, the technician had given me a list of additional resources I might not yet have tried. A call to the Emergency Family Assistance Association revealed a homeless shelter I had not yet heard of, the Atwood Shelter, so I called them. The Atwood Shelter told me that I needed to apply through the Our Center. I told the technician at the Atwood Shelter that I must have made a mistake; we had already applied for every single homeless shelter available through the Our Center. No, she told me; They didn't screen you for the Atwood Center unless you specifically asked. I needed to call the Our Center and make an appointment.

This had been about a week prior, a few days before the ArtWalk. So I called the Our Center up, and requested an appointment.

"These are the documents you will need to bring with you," the receptionist said on the phone. "Your driver's license. Your children's birth certificates. At least three months of pay stubs. Proof of residency."

"Will an eviction notice work?" I interrupted.

"You need proof of where you live now," she told me.

"I don't live anywhere now," I said. "I'm homeless. I'm applying for a homeless shelter."

"You need proof of residency," she said.

"Yeah, but will an eviction notice work? I don't have proof of a residence now. I don't *have* a residence now."

"Where did you sleep last night?" she asked.

"In a broken-down motorhome in a Wal-Mart parking lot." I recited. I had this line memorized almost like my poetry; I just needed to replace a word or two to get the assonance right.

"Where do you get mail?" she asked.

"I don't. I don't get mail. I'm homeless." I said through gritted teeth.

"I'll ask my supervisor. The other documents we will need are proof of any bills you are paying--"

I just laughed.

Now, at the front desk at the Our Center, the receptionist to whom I had spoken on the phone glowered at me while her boss checked me in, checking my passport photo and eviction notice, and Sophie munched happily on her granola bar.

We waited for God with a clipboard to call our name, then we went back into the office of yet another screening technician. This one had a wall covered in miniature children's drawings in pen on quarter-sheets of computer paper. I thought that was smart; cutting the paper into quarters so that the waiting children went through paper slower, but also so that more drawings could fit on the wall. Sophie drew while I answered questions.

First Sophie drew a woman with one head, but two smiles and four eyes. The woman had one dress, a simple triangle, but two sets of arms and two sets of legs-- all stick-figure lines.

"That's very creative," the technician said.

"We've been looking at a lot of Picasso's stuff lately," I said.

I didn't have John's pay stubs from the liquor store; I hadn't been able to find them at the motorhome that morning, or at the shop, and I by the time I got ahold of him by calling him on his mother's phone, we didn't have enough time to drive back to the motorhome and pick up the pay stubs and still make it to the appointment on time.

"I knew I needed them," I told the technician. "I didn't forget them. I just didn't know where they were."

"It's okay," she said. "We can't process your application until we get them, but you can bring them by tomorrow."

The technician gave me tape to hang up two of Sophie's pictures, and she looked over them all-- stick figures holding flowers, a fairy with wings surrounded by crosses meant to represent stars, the words 'SOPHIE' and 'MOMMY.'

"How old is she?" the technician asked. "Four? Five?"

"Three," I said.

"Is she in preschool yet?" the technician asked.

"She will be in the fall."

"So that's all things you've taught her." I felt validated that someone recognized that, but tried to play it off in a more humble manner.

"Well, I mean, I work on stuff with them when I can, at the shop. I try to work on their letters with them every day. And they have a lot of time to just draw."

But I knew, and I know the technician knew, that Sophie wasn't learning all that she could learn. It was painfully obvious that she was intelligent and a quick learner, but still handicapped by her circumstances. She was growing fine in a bookstore, surrounded by books that she wasn't allowed to read because we needed to sell them, practicing her letters and drawing by herself while I attended customers and stocked shelves and filed taxes and sales reports and wrote and wrote and wrote-- but fine is not the same as thriving.

After our appointment, Sophie and I returned to the shop, and I began again with my nervous preparations for the evening. I had now given up hope that John (my husband, not the poet) would be in attendance; when I spoke to him on the phone, he thought he had found someone on Craigslist who would give him a ride to Denver, but it wasn't certain yet. I changed into my new dress: robin's-egg-blue and mid-calf-length. I washed my face in the Old Town Marketplace restroom and replaced my bulky and deteriorating Woody Allen glasses with contacts. I applied make-up, put on jewelry, and painted my nails. I put on deodorant and perfume. I started a pot of coffee. I moved our reclining chair down from the platform in front of the window that we used as a stage; I hoped we would need the extra seating. I arranged all our chairs to face the platform. I moved the coffee table. I set out a vegetable and cheese tray and a tin of fancy cookies. I set out a plastic container of cream puffs, and let Sophie sample one. I sampled one myself, decided they wouldn't stay firm till the end of the night, and put them back in our mini-fridge in the back room, in the compartment near the motor where items meant to be refrigerated often froze.

Lawrence Gladeview and John Dorsey returned just after I poured the pot of coffee into the carafe, and I was glad that I had because they immediately asked for a cup.

"We fell asleep on my living room couch," Lawrence explained. "We were just rehearsing and we must have fallen asleep because we woke up and it was five-thirty so we figured we better get down here."

"Would you like anything else? Help yourselves to the refreshments," I said.

"No, just the coffee," Lawrence said. "I think we're just going to try to perk ourselves up and rehearse a little." John didn't say anything; he seemed a very shy person.

I took Sophie to one of the many empty units in Old Town Marketplace-- the one across the lobby from our unit, with big floor-to-ceiling windows like ours, so that I could keep an eye on her. I turned on the portable DVD player and left her with a snack, and returned to the bookstore.

Lawrence and I started chatting and I explained that John had a 'family emergency' and was on his way back from Kansas but probably wouldn't return in time for the event. I said all this with a very rehearsed smile plastered onto the lower part of my face.

A poet named Jerry Smaldone arrived, along with a long-haired man in his mid-sixties and a Jimi Hendrix t-shirt, whom I later heard Lawrence refer to as Jerry's "handler." Jerry had thick, furry grey eyebrows and he reminded me of my grandfather, if my grandfather had been an Italian from Chicago. Jerry, however, had spent most his life in Colorado. He seemed very calm and relaxed, and genuinely interested in our bookstore and our support of local authors. He had four extra copies of his book, and I printed off our standard consignment contract. He filled it out but left the selling price blank.

"I'm being honest here. I don't care about getting money back from this. I'm here because I love poetry and bookstores."

I smiled and thanked him and wished that my professional politeness would not so often disguise my genuine gratitude.

Marco arrived with his daughter Carmen; he had messaged me earlier that day asking if it was alright if he brought her. I had told him that I would have a movie or something to occupy the children. But he was nervous about her being in the other unit unsupervised, even though it was empty, so I unplugged the DVD player and brought it back to the bookstore and set it up on top of the printer, behind the counter. I started the movie over and set the two miniature children's chairs staggered so that both girls could sit behind the counter and watch the movie. I got them each a cookie and they giggled incessantly.

John Dorsey and Lawrence and Jerry were talking amongst themselves, every so often repeating, "Is Michael coming? Is Mike on his way? Will Mike be here?" It seemed that Michael Adams, the fourth poet in their troupe, had been hospitalized the prior day.

"I figured he'd call if he couldn't make it," Lawrence said. "And he hasn't called yet."

"Well, that either means that he's fine or really bad," Jerry said. I started bringing in extra chairs from the lobby. Dustin and his very tall literary agent arrived, and they took the seats closest to the front of the room. Dustin's mother was not here; usually she would attend events like this, but her homeless-outreach organization was meeting that night with the Longmont Police Department to discuss the homeless problem in Longmont.

Lawrence's wife arrived. She was a pretty woman with long brunette hair; I would guess that both her and Lawrence were in their late twenties or early thirties. Sometimes I was intimidated by the authors and poets who were my clients and only peers, and I felt like a baby at 22. Maybe that's why I liked Dustin; at 17, we were closer in age. There were not many 17-year-old author-publishers or 22-year-old author-entrepreneurs on the literary scene, something I hoped to help change.

Like John and I, Lawrence and his wife had simply decided to pack up their belongings and move to Colorado, although they came from the more cosmopolitan D.C. area and their money had not run out.

Michael Adams soon arrived with his wife, and like many old men, Michael was bald; but when he got closer, I realized that he was missing his eyebrows and eyelashes as well.

"Let me know if I can accommodate anyone with seating or refreshments or anything," I interjected as politely as possible, as Lawrence got Michael a bottle of water and everyone inquired about his health. I was trying to figure out how to ask if Michael would prefer to read sitting down, or needed anything else to make himself comfortable. I for one have never felt like standing up for extended periods of time immediately after being released from the hospital.

Once everyone was satisfied that Michael was still alive, he pulled away to speak to me privately.

"Well... Happy to be here?" I had meant to ask if he was happy to be out of the hospital, but it had somehow come out all wrong. I cursed my tied tongue and social ineptitude and found myself wishing, not for the first or the last time, that John was here. Always charismatic, he had a certain skill at connecting with other people that I could never duplicate.

I printed out a consignment contract for Michael, stepping over the girls to do so.

"You're in our way," Sophie said.

"Shhh," I said.

Michael filled out the contract for one of his books, of

which he had four extra copies, and gave me the contact information for the publisher of his other book, because it needed to be ordered directly from the publisher.

"They will be happy to hear from you," Michael said. "If you order four, that will be a big order for them. They're a mico- micro-press."

"Well, that's what we're here to do," I said. "We want to support the independent press. We can't exactly give them an advantage over the Big Six, but we can sure as hell try."

The men decided to start the event, and Lawrence gave a witty and well-received introduction to which I barely paid attention because I was so nervous. I did, however, learn that John Dorsey was visiting from Toledo, Ohio, to tour the stores around Colorado. He and Lawrence had never met in-person before, until Lawrence picked John up from the airport. John was sleeping on Lawrence's couch. "Crashing" was the term Lawrence used. I wondered what his wife thought about that. They had read at Boulder Bookstore and Innesfree, an exclusively-poetry store, already. I was honored and somewhat mortified that our store was on the tour list along with those giants in the independent bookstore scene.

While the men read, I struggled to keep Sophie and Carmen quiet, and worried about whether there was enough seating and whether I should leave to try to find more. Eight chairs and the couch had been just enough for everyone, except me, when the performance began; but to my delight, a handful of latecomers arrived during the first couple of poems, but that meant that some people had to stand. Jerry Smaldone stood at the back of the store when he was done reading, and he flipped through several books displayed on our shelves while Lawrence read. I would have thought it rude, except that he flipped through the books not hurriedly and out of boredom, but slowly and deliberately as if he were very interested in each individual book he picked up. I felt a certain pride in my carefully curated stock as he browsed.

John Dorsey took the stage with a voice that was almost a

shout; he was accustomed to speaking at Open Mic events, not like our little ones, but big ones at crowded, noisy bookstores and bars where a poet had to project. His poetry was low-brow and a lot of it was about the steel mill where his brother worked, or God's apparent disregard for trailer parks, or a shopkeeper's suicide during a shitty economy. I liked it immediately; it was relatable. Not like like how vague terms like desperation and exhaustion and hope are relatable, but brass tacks, like his eighth-grade shop teacher's gruesome digits, repeatedly sawn off and sewn back on.

I had never taken a shop class and I didn't have to, to be able to relate to that poem. 'Bride of Frankenstein' by John Dorsey. Please do look it up.

After the readings were over, people snacked on the refreshments for a while and congratulated the poets, but nobody bought any book or even browsed, except for the browsing Jerry Smaldone had done during the reading. Before he left, he insisted upon leaving a five-dollar contribution to the bookstore, thanking me again for 'what I was doing.' When authors said this, I had a standard response to dish out: "We couldn't do what we're doing without you doing what you're doing." Meaning writing, publishing, performing, organizing events-- but not, usually, buying books.

I couldn't argue with a five-dollar donation, though.

Lawrence and I talked for a long time after the event; Because Lawrence was giving him a ride, he couldn't leave without John Dorsey, who was engaged in conversation with someone else-- Marco, I think, or maybe Michael or Jerry's handler in the Jimi Hendrix shirt. Lawrence had given us a couple extra copies of each of his poetry books, because we only had one copy left of each.

"They went fast, they're pretty popular," I commented as I stocked the new copues.

"I gave you guys three copies of each, right?" he asked. I nodded, and he laughed raucously, and I was a little sad. Not because he was laughing at us for selling so little volume, but because for a local modern poet, four copies sold *was* pretty popular.

"I think the reason everyone loves what you're doing," Lawrence, "I mean, apart from the sense of community you guys help foster, is that you're making this stuff really approachable. I love it, anyway. I mean, there's some people that don't think accessibility is a good thing. They want to keep this stuff exclusive. And that's just not what the arts are for. They're for everybody, or they're just not worth anything. And, like, all these people giving James Franco flak for getting into poetry, saying he's an actor, not a poet, and he should stick to what he knows-- You didn't hear about that?" Lawrence interrupted himself, apparently sensing from my expression that I didn't know what he was talking about. I shook my head.

"Yeah, so James Franco decided he wants to start supporting poetry, and participating in it. So he's been holding these private readings at his house, like inviting different poets and sponsoring them. John's actually going next week," he said, pointing with his hand across the room at John Dorsey's back.

"James... Franco? Like *the* James Franco?" That was all I could think of to say.

"Yeah, yeah, James Franco." Lawrence grinned.

"You're *shittin'* me!" I shouted.

I could tell Lawrence was really getting a kick out of my reaction, so I calmed down and we talked some more about the importance of getting youth involved in poetry and writing and art. Not *instead* of drinking or drugs, we agreed; just so that they'd have a reason not to screw up their lives by doing too many.

When Lawrence left with John Dorsey, I said good-bye and told John we'd love to have him back again some time.

"I'd love to come back," John said.

"And bring James Franco with you!" I added, blushing as soon as the words left my mouth.

"What?" John asked, looking at Lawrence.

"Oh, yeah, uh, I might have told her that you know James

Franco," Lawrence said.

"Oh, yeah, sure. Like, not right away or anything. But I could probably get him to come in like the next year."

"You're messing with me," I said.

"What?" John asked again. I felt a little bad for teasing someone so shy.

"You-- you're just messing with me now that I know that you know James Franco. You think I'll believe it."

"No, really, I probably could," John said. "We're pretty good friends."

"Really?" I asked. I was afraid to dare to believe it.

"Yeah, another friend introduced us, he's a poet too. He gave James Franco my phone number. James called me up in the middle of the night one night, it was like four in the morning, and I was like, 'Who's this?' and he was like, 'James Franco.'"

"Wow," I said. "What time was it for him?"

"What?"

"What time was it for James Franco where he was? Was it four in the morning there, too?"

"Oh, I have no idea where he was at. Pretty surreal, though, to have James Franco call you at four in the morning."

John and Lawrence left, and so did Marco and Carmen, and Sophie and I went home to our motorhome, and we slept together on Sophie's bed with Rigby.

Four

Wednesday morning, Sophie and I went to breakfast at the Our Center soup kitchen with forty or so others who were homeless or in halfway-houses or maybe just who were poor. About half of them were regulars I recognized, although I didn't know many by name. There was John Redfeather, who said 'Peace!' to everyone he met and not much else. One day a few weeks prior, at lunch with John and Sophie and Lyric, every table was full when John Redfeather came through the line, so my husband John invited him to sit with us. John Redfeather sat politely, eating his food and offering his cookies to the kids, then he suddenly burst out, "I've had some girls tell me I make a pretty good boyfriend." He said this to me. I was embarrassed, mostly for him, because I realized he probably had dementia and didn't realize how old he was.

"I'm sure you are, but she already has a pretty good boyfriend," John my husband said, rescuing me. I was grateful to him for that.

John Redfeather was there at breakfast, and so was a chubby blonde girl who always wore a skirt, even in the snow, and pretended to speak Spanish. There were a lot of Mexican men who laughed at her when she did this, but I didn't recognize any of them specifically. There was an elderly man with a walker, and sometimes his nose dripped into his food. There were quite a few men who were very tan or Hispanic, hard to tell which, that wore leather vests and leather cowboy hats with feathers. Lots wore this uniform. John Redfeather's cowboy hat, on the other hand, was felt, like my husband John's. One man with curly red hair, always reading a pulp science-fiction paperback, had been in the Our Center free clinic one day at the same time as me. A nurse had talked to him about managing his gout while another made lots of phone calls, trying to find a charity that would pay for me to see a doctor because my foot hurt too, and rather than gout, she thought my lupus might be returning from remission. My foot gradually got better, or at least a little less worse, and I never saw a doctor.

The redheaded man was sitting at a table with another man and three other women; overhearing their conversation, I gathered that the other man at the table was visiting from Denver, here in Longmont to see his lady-friend. She was introducing him to everyone around the table.

"This one here's writing a book," she said, indicating the red-haired man. I perked up in my seat to listen closer.

"What's it about?" the other man asked. He wore the leather vest uniform of the homeless who sleep outside, and he had a hiking backpack.

The red-headed man coughed. "Well, it's about being homeless. It's about life homeless here in Colorado." I started debating how to introduce myself.

"Sounds interesting," the other man said. "How far have you gotten?"

The red-haired man coughed again. "Well, I'm actually in the research stage right now." My posture fell. He hadn't written anything yet.

As Sophie and I made our way through the line, a well-dressed man touched my elbow.

"Do you need help carrying her tray?" he asked, and even though I instantly recognized him, all I could stammer was a "No, thanks, I got it."

His name was Chris. He wore khakis and a black dress-shirt, and he carried both a rain jacket and a black felt dress coat, along with an overstuffed black backpack. He was Hispanic and had neatly-trimmed black hair with just a bit of salt-and-pepper in the temple. I had seen him twice before, but it was only now that I put two and two together:

The first time I had seen him, we were newly homeless and didn't have a vehicle to leave Rigby in while we ate breakfast at the Our Center; our truck had broken down our fifth day homeless, and we didn't get the new one until our tax return finally arrived, a month later. It was snowing, then, so John waited with Rigby in the foyer while I ate with the kids. I came to bring John a cup of coffee, but he already had one; Chris, a stranger to us then, had brought him a cup. When I was done eating, I took John's place with Rigby so John could go inside and get some breakfast, and Rigby had a bowl of water out in front of her; Chris had brought it as well. He stopped by one more time while I sat with Rigby, asking if I needed anything. I didn't. Then one of the attendants, probably a volunteer, stopped me to ask if Rigby was a licensed medical dog. I lied and said yes, but we hightailed it out of there soon after.

The second time I saw Chris, I didn't recognize him. Anyone would be guilty of this. I might blame others for it, but everyone does it, myself included. I saw Chris somewhere where I didn't expect a homeless person to be, so I assumed he wasn't homeless. So, I didn't recognize him.

I didn't recognize that he was homeless because he walked into our shop.

He was well-dressed in his clean khakis and neat haircut, and he didn't have his backpack with him; his felt dress coat was over his arm. I put on my smile, genuinely excited to have a rare browser in our shop, optimistic I might make a sale. I greeted him and told him about our shop. He asked questions and picked up quite a few books, but put them back. He asked about our 'Free Wifi' sign.

"Oh, yeah, we have wifi and we encourage customers to sit and hang out, work on their computers, whatever. We also offer free coffee in exchange for checking in on Facebook or Twitter." I had a robotic script for this offer, too. I had rehearsed it so often.

"Oh, I just have my tablet so I can't do that right now. I

spend a lot of time at the library." He looked at the coffee carafe.

"Honestly I'd probably just give you a cup if you wanted. Just tell a friend about us or something." I grinned. He shook his head. I was trying to make it sound like he'd still be doing us a favor. I had no idea he was homeless, but I was starting to recognize him.

"I'm pretty sure I know you from somewhere," I said. "Didn't you say you were a journalist?"

"Yeah, back in D.C.," he said. "Not around here."

"Wichita?" I asked. He shook his head.

"Did you used to be--" I pantomimed taking a picture because I couldn't think of the word for a photojournalist.

"No, not really. Listen, I gotta go but thanks for talking. I'll come back when I have money. Good luck," he said, and he walked out of the store with his coat.

Later that day he posted on our bookstore's Facebook page: "By far the most impressive bookstore in Longmont, possibly Boulder county. Love their author resources and coffee." That was how I knew his name. I had done some mild stalking on his Facebook page, and saw some pictures of a black pit bull, and others of Chris in a newsroom in the '70's. His hair was fashionably long then.

Now, in the food pantry line, I recognized Chris in all his incarnations: Kind homeless man, former journalist, bookstore patron. One and the same person. And all I could do was stutter a thanks.

After Sophie and I returned to the shop, I looked Chris up on Facebook again. Definitely the same guy. I sent him a message: "Well, I guess I realized where I recognized you from. Ha ha. Except it's not very funny."

A few minutes later he replied: "Why isn't it funny? Because we're homeless?" He must have been at the library, which was directly across the alleyway from Old Town Marketplace. So I wasn't much surprised at all that he stopped in a few minutes later.

"Hey," I greeted him, grinning.

"Hi," he said. "How are you guys? What's John doing?"

"He's in Denver," I said. I had gotten a call from him earlier that morning. "He's stuck there till two. John and Lyric went to John's sister's graduation in Wichita and they got in to Denver before noon. No bus to Longmont till two. I hope he's back soon."

"No kidding," Chris said. "I kinda hate Denver."

"Me, too."

"Do you guys come to the Our Center every morning for breakfast?" he asked.

"Not quite every morning," I said, "but we don't have much space to keep food cold or anywhere to cook, so it's nice for getting a warm meal. The H.O.P.E. people bring sack meals out to where the RV's are parked every night, and they're a lot healthier but they're almost always cold."

"Yeah, they distribute at six in the Park-n-Ride parking lot too."

"Is that where you stay?" I asked.

"I stay in a variety of places," he said.

"I'm sorry if that was too intrusive," I said, genuinely concerned that I had offended him. "I'm still getting the hang of homeless etiquette."

"It's okay. The homeless are the one class of people that you can ask anything. Usually I try to stay awake most of the night in a fast food place or Winchell's," he said, naming a local donut shop. "The last couple of nights, I've stayed in the rear doorway of the Tex-Mex bar."

I thought we were lucky to have the kids, then; they made a lot of things harder because they were always the exact opposite of inconspicuous, which is what a homeless person has to be in order to survive. But they also meant that we had to find somewhere to sleep every night. And that meant that John and I had somewhere to sleep, too. We were spared a lot of the staying-up-all-night-in-a-fast-food-joint experience by having kids.

"Jeez," I said. "We've been pretty lucky so far because we had a tent when we were evicted in March. We mostly just set it up in the fairgrounds after the attendant left for the night, and took it down before the new one got there in the morning."

"Yeah, a lot of people do the tent thing," Chris said.

"If you want to borrow one, we don't need it any more right now. We still fantasize, though, that someday we won't be homeless any more and we'll be people who camp for fun again."

"I have those same dreams..." Chris trailed off. "Thanks for the offer, but for me, it doesn't work. People come and tell you to move along or write you a ticket if they recognize you and know you're homeless. Or if people see me in a tent, then when they see me around town they won't let me sit in their coffee shop all afternoon."

That was another thing that having children protected us from. Everyone assumed we weren't homeless. We were a family camping. We were a family dirty after playing in the mud or going on a hike. We were a family showering at the rec center after a game of basketball or before we swam. Everyone assumes that if you're a family, you must not be homeless, because no one likes to think that families can be homeless. No one likes to think that *their* family could have been homeless.

Everyone's much more comfortable with family-less people being homeless.

"People try to run you off if they think you're homeless," Chris went on. "They don't want us around."

"It's really stupid," I said. "The homeless people around here have been nicer to us than anyone else. Except the H.O.P.E. people."

"But we're still a scourge. We remind people that poverty exists. They don't like that."

"The fuckin' newspaper, man," I said. "The Times-Call is the worst. They're so biased. All that shit they published about homeless people making downtown unsafe for business owners. It really pisses me off."

"Yeah, they're not exactly the most professional newspaper in the world," Chris added. I wondered if, as an unemployed journalist, he resented those writers.

"I've written them letters about being homeless and how biased everyone is, but they don't publish it. They don't want to hear it. I've written the City Council, too. No one ever responds."

"Well, good for you for writing. It's a shame they won't report objectively."

"The homeless people don't bother anyone here, for the most part. They've been really nice to us."

"Some can be."

"Ya know what happened when we first got the RV? It was during that really bad snowstorm at the beginning of May. We were parked over at the other Wal-Mart on 119 and we had to be really careful about people seeing us, so we only went there after dark. So we were staying at the McDonald's till the PlayPlace closed at nine, and when they turned the lights off, all the homeless guys came in to charge their cell phones. We were getting the kids' shoes on and one of the homeless guys came over to us and he was like, 'I've seen you guys around at the Our Center, I know you guys are homeless, do you and your kids have somewhere to stay tonight?' and John told them we did, because we had the RV, and they told us that they had somewhere that didn't have heat or electricity, but if we needed somewhere to stay the night, we were welcome to it. I don't know where they were staying, but it couldn't have been much more than the RV. Still, they were willing to share it. We didn't even know them."

"Yeah, for the most part, people are pretty willing to look out for one another," Chris said. "Just be careful who you trust."

"I know," I said.

"Do you know why I'm up here?" Chris asked. "What happened?" I couldn't tell if he was trying to change the subject, or if was a continuation of our conversation.

"I don't," I said.

"My girlfriend, Jodi, and I lived in D.C. We moved to Cali, but it didn't work out, so she moved here. I stayed. I met a woman. Crystal. I never heard from Jodi; she never answered my calls, never returned them. So I moved on. With Crystal. We were going to move East for work, but when we got there, she decided it was too cold. I burned a lot of bridges getting those jobs and not taking them, so we were fighting a lot. She wanted to go back to her ex, so she called him. So I said, 'Fine, I'm calling Jodi.' I didn't expect her to answer, because she had never answered. But she did that time. We were in Austin, Texas, then, and Crystal got mad and took off. She left me with the clothes on my back and my backpack."

"Jeez... Rough stuff," I said. I didn't know what else to say.

"I decided to come to Longmont to reconnect with Jodi, and we were both excited. But when I got here, Jodi shot and killed herself."

I felt my jaw drop. "Oh my god... I'm so sorry to hear that," I managed to say.

"I've been grieving ever since. When it first happened, I did some really stupid stuff that got me in a lot of trouble. I just... wanted to be with her." He said pointedly, smiling and offering his hands forward in a sad shrug.

"That's... understandable," I said. "I'm sorry that happened to you."

He shrugged. "I just want to keep a low profile now. I made myself too recognizable around town. Hey, are you guys hungry?"

"What? No, I'm all right." His sudden change in conversation threw me off.

"Are you sure? Let me buy you guys lunch. People like us have to watch out for each other."

"No, it's okay, I've eaten." I pointed to a microscopic, empty tuna salad tin on the coffee table. It had came in a bag from H.O.P.E. I had just finished it when Chris walked in.

"What about Sophie?"

"She's eaten, too."

"I've got food stamps and I'm headed up to the gas station. At least let me get you a Gatorade. You guys are stuck here all day and can't leave." I hesitated. "I'm going to go get you something. Do you mind if I leave my backpack? It's heavy to carry."

Chris left and I put his backpack in the back room. He returned forty minutes later with a chicken-salad sandwich for me and a ham sandwich for himself, and a Lunchable for Sophie. He had a fruit punch Gatorade for himself, and strawberry lemonade for me, and Sophie's Lunchable came with a Capri Sun. I wondered if he got me chicken salad because he assumed from the tuna salad that that was what I preferred. In truth, I hate anything with mayonnaise, and I felt terrible for thinking about that. But even with my aversion for meat salads, the sandwich tasted extraordinarily satisfying, probably because it was the freshest food I'd eaten in months. I was still wearing my robin's-egg-blue dress from the previous evening, hoping for John to see me in it when he returned because I thought I looked halfway decent for once, but I got a little mayonnaise on my dress and I was very cross at myself for that.

"Sorry it took so long, I ran into an old friend at the gas station. This little girl that used to follow me around when I first moved here... She's funny. She's selling drugs now. I don't like that. But she hadn't eaten so I had to get her something. She's like my little sister, ya know?"

Chris finished his sandwich before I did; I've always been a slow eater. He wiped his mouth politely.

"Could I use your phone?" he said. "I got an interview with Home Depot and I'm supposed to call them back."

I shook my head and retrieved the cell phone for him, and while Chris was on the phone, John walked into the store, with Lyric trailing behind.

"You act like I've been gone forever," John laughed, as I finally released our embrace.

"It feels like it," I said. I picked Lyric up.

Chris left soon after, and then John went to the bathroom to wash his face and wipe himself down with paper towels, and then he changed shirts and went to his second-shift job at the liquor store, and I was alone with the kids again.

John came home late at night, and we curled up in our

usual embrace that cannot be described to anyone who has not felt John's heartbeat through his chest, transfixed by the spell of meeting again after a long absence.

Thursday morning, I had an early appointment with Housing and Human Services to determine whether or not we would be eligible for food stamps. I extricated myself carefully from the bed, so as not to wake John or the kids, and I took John's driver's license from his wallet and left two dollars and fifty cents for the bus ride for John and the kids. I took Rigby with me in the truck, because she couldn't ride the bus. I let John and the children sleep; especially John, because it seemed he'd gotten about seven hours of sleep, total, the previous two nights, between the Greyhound bus and second shift at the liquor store.

I waited on a vinyl chair in the county office for God with a clipboard, thumbing through my folder while I waited. Birth certificates, immunization records, John's driver's license, my passport; I had no driver's license. John's pay stub from Francis Street Liquors. Our sales reports from the bookstore for February, March, and April. A copy of our rental agreement with Old Town Marketplace. We had been denied for food stamps twice before, for not having enough documentation. I was nervous. A handyman repaired a broken door in the foyer of the office building. An old man begged and wheezed at the receptionist's desk for a status update on his insurance application. There was vomit on the carpet by the puzzles and blocks meant for waiting children. But there weren't any children yet this morning so I didn't do anything about it. The appointment was uneventful.

John called me after the appointment. He was taking the kids to the park before coming to the shop, and I regretted not leaving Rigby with them, but he said that wouldn't have worked anyway because they were taking the bus to the park. I didn't blame them; it was about a mile's walk from Wal-Mart.

"Oh, and one more thing," John said before I hung up. "We got an eviction notice on our RV this morning."

"Are you serious?" I asked. "When?"

"After you left. About ten o'clock this morning. It says we

have till ten tomorrow to move the RV."

"Oh, shit," I said. "Will the truck be able to do it?" It was running again, thanks to the new power-steering belt, but the brakes were essentially non-existent and the wheels made this horrid metal-on-metal sound that we assumed was due to the alignment.

"I don't know... With how heavy the motorhome is, we might not have wheels any more if we try to tow it."

"Are we gonna do it today?"

"No, we can do it tomorrow morning before work," John said.

I wondered what the eviction process would look like; although Billy's camper-trailer was now gone, there was one other motor-less camper-trailer still parked in our alcove, and ours was certainly not the only one of the motorhomes and vehicles that didn't run. I wondered if it would be like the evictions of gypsies from campsites in courtyards and fields outside cities in Europe. I wondered if everyone would go quietly, downtrodden and humiliated like a dog with its tail between its legs, or if people would be angry and the police would come.

Later that day, we were approved for food stamps, much to my relief. John worked second shift at the liquor store again, so I closed the shop and took the kids to Wal-Mart, where I let Sophie and Lyric each pick out whatever fresh fruit they wanted-- Lyric picked cherries and Sophie picked a nectarine-- and I bought refreshments for our event Friday. I bought Pop-Tarts for John, and protein bars. We couldn't buy anything perishable because we didn't have any way to keep food cold at our motorhome, but I got a miniature single-serving tub of ice cream for each of the children and I, to the children's delight. I was pretty sure they deserved it after all they'd been through.

We got strange looks from the cashier, but I was confident she'd seen people come through her line with weirder stuff before-- It *was* Wal-Mart, after all. For the first time in almost a month we had lived in the Wal-Mart parking lot, I pushed a shopping cart of groceries to our home.

I unlocked the motorhome door and let the children in, and then I started unloading the groceries. While I was doing this, a man stepped out of his motorhome on the opposite side of the alcove, and started walking towards me. He was large, in the poor-fat-man's uniform of a sweat-stained t-shirt and sweat shorts, and he had cavities in most of his teeth.

"Hey," I said when he got close enough to hold a conversation.

"Hey," he replied. "I saw you guys got one of the notices and, well, you look new." I wondered what that meant-- probably that I still had all my teeth. "I just wanted to let you know, you don't need to worry or freak out or nothin.' They won't, like, come out here and tow ya. Usually if you just talk to the management, they'll give ya a couple extra days. These guys aren't too bad."

"Oh... well, thanks," I said.

"Just didn't want ya guys worrying."

"Thanks for that. I mean... I didn't even know you could get evicted from Wal-Mart. I got this and I was like, wow, first we got evicted from an apartment, then we got evicted from a hotel, and now we're evicted from Wal-Mart... I'm not exactly moving up in the world." I laughed.

"I hear ya," he said. "My wife and I were livin' out of that car for five years before we got the RV." He pointed at a maroon sedan parked next to his motorhome. I laughed nervously.

"Take care," he said, and he walked away again.

Shellshocked, I went inside the motorhome to eat my ice cream before it melted. I wondered where we would be living in five years.

It's a bit funny how we came to live in a motorhome in the first place. It's not funny at all, but it's a story I can tell like a joke.

What do you do with four thousand dollars from your newly-arrived tax return, and an eviction on your credit history? You stay fucking homeless, because no one will rent to you, no matter how much money you hand them.

Ha ha. Okay, here's another one:

Four people drive to Fort Lupton to buy an RV for eight hundred dollars. Two miles out of Fort Lupton, the RV dies at the top of a hill. The family goes back to the RV's owner and they say, 'Hey, you sold us a shitty RV. We want our money back.' The previous owners take a look at the RV, and the engine's choked. A valve needs replaced. The family gets their money back and drives back to Longmont. Two days later, they drive to Brighton to pick up a different RV for a thousand dollars. They make it five miles out of town when the RV dies, again at the top of a hill. The family goes back to the dealer and says, 'Hey, you sold us a shitty RV. We want out money back.' The dealer says no dice, you bought it, you're stuck with it. The engine, radiator, and batteries are all toast. The RV needs to be rewired. It will cost thousands of dollars.

And here's the punch line:

A valve costs about fifty dollars.

I don't like stories like that. I don't memorize stories by their punch lines. I write poetry, because that's what I can write while I'm on the side of a highway, trying to string together words while semi-trailers zip by and the gust of hot wind picks up my skirt and prairie dogs bark at me and the kids fight in the cab of the truck while John leans down under the hood of a Dodge Sportsman while steam billows and hot oil burns his fingers and splatters my calves. I'm not there at all, I'm stringing words together in my head, while John and I fight over whether we will sleep in the slanted motorhome, resting at a tilt because it's parked halfway off the side of the highway and half on the steep ditch, shaking every time a car passes, or whether we will pay sixty dollars for a motel in Brighton, or whether we will sleep in the truck in a parking lot, or whether we will leave the RV behind and drive back to Longmont to sleep in the bookstore, or whether we will pay a hundred and fifty dollars for a tow. I'm lying awake in bed in a motel room, writing poetry, writing my masterpieces in my head, instead of wondering whether John is slashing tires at the car lot where we bought our RV or finishing off a bottle of whiskey under a bridge or when he's coming back or if he's coming back at all. I've checked out of the situation completely, though my entire body's weight is on the brake pedal, my fingers clenched and white on the steering wheel, my thigh is ignoring the sting of a yellow jacket, my body steers the RV, trailing behind five feet of tow chains and the back of John's truck, terrified of his rear bumper. My mind is not there. It is busy thinking of nouns and verbs and stories I can use instead of adjectives like lonely and desperate.

Five

Friday, we left a note on our motorhome door: "Can't get a tow till Saturday. Please give us an extra day. Please call John before towing," and our phone number.

We didn't have time to mess with the motorhome Wal-Mart eviction ordeal on Friday; we had another author event that evening, and I was terrified. Gail Storey was probably the biggest-name author we'd ever had at our store, and if we didn't have a big crowd for her, I would probably die of humiliation. We needed to spend our entire day preparing for the event, or at least worrying about it. Additionally, our wheels were still making that horrid metal-on-metal sound, and though it may have just been the brakes, we were still terrified that towing something as heavy at the motorhome would permanently damage our alignment or bearings or some other parts that I was unfamiliar with, but John made it sound like it was very bad.

We had lots to do before Gail Storey's event at six: Namely, getting showers, which was a very long process. It had been a full week since our showers the previous Friday, before the ArtWalk.

On my way back from the showers with Sophie, a woman stopped us for directions.

"Do you know how to get Coffman from here?" she asked. Her hair was brushed and she looked clean enough to not be homeless; but then, so did Sophie and I with our still-wet hair. I looked around for a minute before answering.

"Uh, I believe we *are* on Coffman," I said. The rec center and the main bus terminal were both at the corner of Eighth and

Coffman, and Sophie and I were walking south on Coffman, back towards the shop.

"Oh, darn. So I need to go that way?" she gestured vaguely. Her eyes didn't quite focus on anything.

"Where are you trying to go?" I asked politely.

"I'm from Montana. I've never rode the bus before. I got it all mixed up," she said

I laughed. "We came from a city that didn't have public transportation either. It takes a while to get it figured out."

"I came from over at Seventeenth and Pace, but I think I got off at the wrong stop," she said.

"Where are you trying to get, again?" I asked. I thought I might genuinely be able to help her, at least if her destination was within walking distance or on the 323 or 324 lines, which were what we took the most often.

"I just... I just had to stop and talk to you. Your daughter is so precious. She reminds me so much of my baby girl. My baby passed away. Your daughter's just so precious."

"Oh... I'm so sorry to hear that," I said. I didn't know what else to say so I let Sophie tell the lost, child-like woman about her flowers and her dog, and the woman was happy to hear about it all.

"I have to go now," she said suddenly, after tenderly petting Sophie's wet hair. She turned around and went back the way she came, towards the bus terminal.

Sophie and I headed back towards the book store, and John wondered why we took so long but he was placated by my reply.

Aside from taking showers and trying to make ourselves look presentable, John and I spent most of the day trying to figure out whether the event was advertised well enough. We had passed out fliers at the ArtWalk the prior Friday, and we had wanted to hang up fliers at the local coffee shops and community college campus during the week, but we either hadn't had the time, or I had been to busy trying to run the shop and attend appointments by myself while John was gone. We had submitted the event to the newspaper, but we didn't know if they had published anything about it or not. If I had been less distracted, I might have remembered the old woman at the ArtWalk telling me she read about the event in the newspaper, but it failed to come to mind, if that tells you anything about our mental state at the time. Moreover, we had plenty of reason to believe the Times-Call wouldn't publish anything about us.

Chris was absolutely correct about the unprofessionalism of the Times-Call; one of our other authors, Robert Miller, had referred to it as "the Chamber of Commerce newsletter." That wasn't quite right, though. It was the City Council who had the Times-Call in their pocket. At one time, the Longmont City Council had been comprised entirely of Klu Klux Klan members, or so the story goes, and in my opinion, we, as a city, hadn't progressed much beyond that point. As best as I could tell, the City Council were a bunch of old white guys who were completely out-of-touch with real life, the way other people lived it. Recently, the city of Longmont had voted to allow recreational marijuana dispensaries; the City Council had then vetoed the effort, citing their greater ability to understand what the voters of Longmont really wanted than the voters themselves.

In April, the City Council had began its crusade to end services to the homeless, citing that they attracted a "homeless problem" to Longmont. We found out about this crusade one day at work when a preppy Latina woman walked into our bookstore with a clipboard. We were, as a general rule, wary of people with clipboards.

"Hi, I own Santiago's at First and Main, and I've been going around to business owners downtown Longmont to ask them to sign this petition." She held out the clipboard.

"What's the petition for?" John asked. Once every couple months, a new business owner came around with a petition for their neighbors; a certain number of signatures were required for new businesses to be able to obtain a liquor license. But Santiago's was not new.

"The Well wants to put an addiction treatment center at

Second and Main, and this would cause trouble for all of us. The addicts and homeless people it will attract will scare our customers and undoubtably cause safety concerns for our employees."

John and I stared at her tight-lipped. She still held out the clipboard, but we didn't take it.

"This petition is for business owners who are opposed to The Well opening its center. The City Council is having a meeting Thursday evening and we want to present this petition to show how many businesses are opposed to the center opening around our businesses."

John continued to stare icily at her. I was openly glaring. She apparently realized that she wasn't getting anywhere with us; she started back-peddling.

"I mean, we all go through rough times. I know that. I even have family... but what I mean is, yes I feel bad for these people, but the addiction treatment center shouldn't be somewhere like this where it affects other businesses. I mean, you guys have kids to support. You need your business to succeed. Not homeless people making it harder for you to attract customers. I have nothing against the addiction center. Just somewhere other than here."

"When is that meeting again?" John asked, and she fell silent. She handed him a flyer and walked out.

John went to the City Council meeting that chilly Thursday in April, and I waited with the kids at the shop because we had no where else to wait. We would sleep on the floor again that night. John had done his research, beforehand: The branch that The Well wanted to open at Second and Main would only be an administrative office, possibly housing intake. No actual treatment would take place at that location. Still, no one wanted it near them. John was going to the meeting as a business owner, not a homeless person, because he wanted to be persuasive; also because, after our picture had been in Longmont Magazine, he couldn't risk anyone recognizing him and finding out that the bookstore owners were homeless.

He rehearsed his points before the meeting: That rehabilitating homeless addicts and returning them to working positions in our community would enhance our overall economy, improving business for everyone; even if the homeless themselves never became patrons of our store or Santiago's, specifically, if they could be rehabilitated enough even to buy groceries in Longmont, it would improve the economy and business for everyone. That removing the homeless from view did not get rid of the homeless problem. That a centralized location was vital to the success of the program, and that placing the administrative center somewhere hidden from view would further hinder addicts' ability to seek treatment. That it was somewhat hypocritical of the city of Longmont to pretend they support the arts and want to become an artsier community, while simultaneously hiding from view the homeless and addicts, as the artists and the vagabonds are two groups of people who often intersect.

John wound up scrapping that last point because Longmont was only interested in the artists who were wealthy, or at least fully integrated into society, whose art wouldn't make the wealthy citizens of Longmont uncomfortable in any way. As we saw it, there were two problems with Longmont's pickiness: The first is that it was impossible for artists to actually support themselves, unless people bought art. And people in Longmont never really did. And the second was that with a clear preference for wealthy artists-- and I am including authors and poets in the category of artists-- only the wealthy artists got to tell their story. Only one point of view was shared. The lack of diversity in art in Longmont was overwhelming.

John returned from the City Council meeting dejected. He had stood up and said his piece. The woman from Santiago's had glared at him. And then the City Council had voted to deny The Well a permit to open offices at Second and Main.

The newspaper, also, told things from only one point of view. They reported on The Well's denied permit, and they quoted a lot of business owners; all of them said they were afraid of the homeless people who made Longmont so dangerous at night. They didn't come to interview us. They did interview the Catholic Bookstore owner, who rented the window-front unit next to ours in Old Town Marketplace. She specifically said that the drunken homeless people who entered the Marketplace made her afraid for her safety. This struck us as odd, not only because we weren't interviewed or even approached by the newspaper, while she was, right next door, but also because the only drunken people who ever entered Old Town Marketplace were those who spilled in from the upscale bar next door, and John-- but the escaped bar patrons were plenty wealthy. The only homeless people we had ever seen in Old Town Marketplace were ourselves.

There was also a quote from the upscale bar next door, saying that the homeless people left too many cigarette butts outside their door.

"I wonder how they tell the difference between the cigarette butts that belong to homeless people and the cigarette butts that belong to paying customers," John said. And I thought that was very profound. We all have the same dirty cigarette butts in life, no matter what our circumstances. Except that I don't smoke.

After that newspaper article, John started approaching the dirty people who stood on the street outside our window-front and inviting them in for a cup of coffee. I think he did it just to piss off the Catholic Bookstore lady. A homeless man named Josh, always recognizable in his sweat-stained forrest-green t-shirt, set up camp in front of our window-front, smoking cigarettes and eating pudding from a brown paper sack from the H.O.P.E. van. John waited until he was gone, then went outside and picked up his trash.

I started writing the City Council and the newspaper, especially after they decided to shut H.O.P.E. down, too. Dustin's mother couldn't be at the Poetry Tour with Lawrence Gladeview, because that day, the Times-Call had printed another article about how H.O.P.E. attracted homeless people, and she was furiously delegating damage control, which included the meeting with the

Longmont Police Department.

"You never publish my letters," I wrote the Times-Call from an email address that wouldn't give away my name. "You never publish the letters of any homeless people. You never quote them. Would you write an article about teachers in Longmont without interviewing a single teacher? Would you write an article about a Republican candidate while only quoting Democrats?"

They didn't publish that one because it was too vindictive and angry. Or maybe because they knew I was right and they were ashamed. Either way, I never got a response. I wondered if it was because I hadn't included a name, even though I had explained in every letter that outing myself as homeless would risk my employment. I didn't tell them I owned a business. Then it probably would have been too easy for them to figure out.

So we weren't too optimistic about getting a write-up in the newspaper; even with the covert nature of letters, we were still well-known proponents of H.O.P.E. and critics of the newspaper's lack of objectivity. After the televised City Council meeting, John's face was recognizable as an enemy of both City Council and the Times-Call.

And with an author as famous as Gail Storey, we were concerned about not having a write-up in the newspaper. Her publicist had scheduled the book-signing with us; she was the only author who had done an event with us so far who had her own publicist. We knew we owed her more advertising than we had been able to do. I had, however, bought excellent refreshments for the event; after we wrung our hands for most of the afternoon, I set out a fresh fruit tray and trail mix, which I thought appropriate for the subject matter of her book, and a bowl of bite-sized Toblerones. Throughout Gail's memoir of hiking the six-month-long Pacific Crest Trail with her husband, Porter, one of them was always eating a Toblerone. Gail had been forced to leave the trail halfway through due to weight loss and malnutrition, and a medically-prescribed feast of Toblerones allowed her to gain enough weight to rejoin her husband on the trail.

Toblerones had been my father's favorite chocolate when I was a kid, and I had always gotten them for him for Father's Day and his birthday. So I had a special fondness for Toblerones, as well; a certain propensity to view them as a meaningful gift. We had the bowl of bite-sized Toblerones on the coffee table for guests, as well as four full-size candy bars. One, John set up on a display table, along with Gail Storey's book and a trail of polished river pebbles we had bought for a gold-mining activity for children at another author's book-signing. I thought the display looked very simple and elegant.

Twenty minutes before six, we were prepared; Our anxiety had made us early. However, our preparation was rewarded as a couple, and then a single man, entered the store.

"The Gail Storey event?" the man asked. We said yes and he looked around the store for a bit, while six other people arrived and took seats. Dustin and his girlfriend arrived; I was always happy to see them. John started bringing in extra chairs from the lobby.

"I've got another engagement, but will you tell Gail I stopped by?" The man handed me a business card before he left. He was a lawyer. He didn't buy anything.

At six, every chair was full; we had brought in all the chairs from the lobby, so we started on the bar stools that had been left behind in an empty unit when the tenant couldn't pay rent and was forced out of business. Some were broken, but with six more chairs, still people stood. And Gail Storey had not arrived yet.

People started getting impatient; I addressed the crowd and apologized for starting late. "And please help yourself to the refreshments. Coffee, water, and lemonade are over here. Let me know if the temperature needs to be adjusted."

A few minutes later someone let me know that it was too hot at the front of the store; our windows faced west, and the setting sun peered directly into the seating area. With nearly thirty bodies packed into the room, and our broken swamp-cooler, it was certainly toasty. The swamp-cooler technician had came to turn it on the week before, but upon finding it was broken, had notified our landlord and given her an estimate. She, of course, had done nothing.

I brought out a fan from the back room and started debating where to place it; the cord wasn't long, and the outlets were limited. Plugging it in behind the couch would require climbing over people.

"Excuse me. I can't have the fan on me. I can't stand fans," a woman sitting in the front informed me.

"Can I have a show of hands? Who is hot and wants the fan on them?" I asked. About ten people sitting around and behind the anti-fan woman raised their hands. I plugged the fan in at the outlet on our platform in front of the window, and turned the rotating mechanism off. I pointed it slightly downwards so as not to affect the sensitive customer. I returned to the back of the room to wait for Gail. The sensitive woman in front of the fan got up and left.

Just then, I spotted Gail and Porter outside the store. John went to greet them and help carry bags of books, while I resumed crowd control. John was soon stacking books on the back counter. Outside the store, Gail donned a human-sized version of her book cover, printed on a box like a sandwich board advertisement, and a plastic princess tiara. She marched into the store, arms held high, to cheers from our small and crammed audience. Porter, her husband, followed quietly behind, bags of books in hand.

Relieved that the show had begun, I helped John arrange the books on the back counter. In addition to her latest book, the memoir around which this event was centered, Gail had written two novels. However, her memoir came from an independent publisher that specialized in mountaineering, and we were able to order four copies in advance without compromising our morals. We sold one the very day they arrived. We had sold a second to the very prim lady before the ArtWalk, and we had two copies left. Gail's other books, while from an independent publisher as well, came from a larger company out-of-state that required a minimum order and credit application. Luckily, Gail understood our situation and offered to bring her novels to carry on consignment the day of the event. Although her publicist had scheduled the event, Gail herself had contacted us about carrying her books in our store. She had read about us in the Colorado Author's League newsletter, and was excited about our bookstore and our intentions, as so many authors were.

I helped John arrange the novels while Gail introduced herself and her book; Usually I would be rapt by an author's presentation, especially one like Gail's, but I had already read the book, and thus didn't need the primer; additionally, I knew John was under pressure to make our counter look as professional as possible, especially since it was only an old bookshelf pretending to be a counter. I wanted to help not so much because I thought John needed it, but because I knew it would make him feel less stressed about the display.

Once the books were attractively displayed and we were sure they wouldn't bend or warp, John and I stood at the back of the crowd to listen. Dustin was standing near us and gave us a small wave.

Gail told about her adventures on the trail while her audience laughed enthusiastically. The friend of Porter's mother, the old lady who had purchased Gail's book the day of the ArtWalk, was seated in our most stately second-hand over-stuffed armchair. She reminded me a little of Margaret Atwood. I shifted from one side of the room to the other, taking pictures for our website.

After the presentation, Gail took questions from the crowd, and Porter stood, tall and humble, at the back of the room. Dustin and his girlfriend and John and I also lurked there.

"Did you have your packages waiting at check-points ahead of time? Or did you, like, mail them out staggered? Did you mail them all out at once?" a middle-aged woman in sunglasses asked.

"That's a very good question," Gail said, making it sound as though it really was. "We packed all of the boxes ahead of time, but left them open with an inch or two of space on top. That way, we could let our friends know if we needed anything added before they mailed out the boxes. Mostly food requests, once we had been on the trail a while and knew what we were sick of. We had to let them know about two weeks ahead of time, to give them time to ship the boxes before we reached the check point. Next question?"

"How heavy was your pack?" someone asked.

"About seven pounds, plus food and water. Porter's was nine, until I tore my ligament in my knee, and then he added some of my pack to his and I think it weighed about thirteen pounds?" She directed her question to Porter in the back, who nodded in authoritative affirmation.

A neatly-dressed and powdered woman on the couch raised her hand.

"Yes, Anne," Gail said, and I realized that a lot of the wealthy members of the audience were friends of Gail's.

"Did you ever feel like you were in danger with the other hikers? Were you ever scared of people on the trail? Like, of any of the people you met?" She asked. John and I exchanged a look and rolled our eyes.

"No, no, not really," Gail replied. "There's an incredible sense of camaraderie on the trail. I never felt in danger at all-- from the people, anyway. The trail was very dangerous. But even though you might not see another hiker all day, we're all pretty much in the same place on the trail, so if I sat down for a bit, it wouldn't be an hour before someone else would come along. Like if I got hurt or anything. So I felt very safe."

John leaned in close to me and whispered, "How much do you think a gun weighs, compared to their seven-ounce tent? Fucking paranoid bohemian bourgeoisie." The alliterative insult referenced a used book we carried; although the book was pro bo-bo, insisting that their class would save our world, John had adopted the term as an insult.

"How much money did it cost? Sorry if that's too personal... How much would it cost one to hike the PCT? How about that?" Dustin asked that question I had been curious about, but been too embarrassed to ask. I wondered if he was inspired to add a hiking experience to his upcoming transient tour.

"Very inexpensive," Porter cut in, answering before Gail could. "If you sell your car and your house. You lose all of your expenses. You don't have bills to pay or gas to buy. You're not eating out at restaurants all the time. We saved a lot of money."

I was a little irritated at Porter, because Dustin may have been mature for his age, but he sure looked seventeen. Porter should have been able to see that, too; he should have known that Dustin didn't have a house or car to sell. I hated people who classified certain experiences, like taking six months to hike from Mexico to Canada, as experiences that were exclusive to the rich. Realistically, I knew that this was true. If luxury experiences like sleeping in a bed every night or having three solid meals every day were exclusive only to certain classes of people, then why should just anyone get to take off from their job and turn their lives over to where the world is uninhabited?

"You can plan on about a dollar or two per mile," Gail said, breaking in. I was grateful for her more practical advice; at my estimation, that was about six thousand dollars. However, I *was* a little skeptical that would be enough for all the micro-weight gear, tents, sleeping bags, bear canister, water jugs, clothing, as well as new running shoes every three weeks and enough dehydrated food to last for six months. "You definitely have to save up for it. Porter's right, it's less money when you don't have all your daily expenses, eating out and shopping and stuff. But when you do come to an outpost that's a town, you really do want to get to go eat. It makes a difference. It can be done on different budgets, and there were kids doing it who had nothing extra. They couldn't go to an all-you-can-eat buffet in every town, and Porter and I could. Even with that, I still lost too much weight, so I don't know how some of those kids did it. They were sleeping six or ten to a hotel room so that they could all get a shower in the morning. If you're only in town every three weeks or so, it makes a difference if you can rest for a day. You get your stamina back up. A lot of these kids couldn't do that. They also didn't get to have as much meal variety. We had all kinds of dehydrated food, and Porter is a fantastic outdoors cook." Porter bowed his head and smiled at Gail's compliment. I rather liked their relationship, in spite of Porter's sectarian classism. On the other hand, I was sure he didn't mean to exclude any specific groups; he was just genuinely unaware that people existed who had so little money that saving six thousand dollars for a six-month vacation could be such a hardship.

"Yes, John," Gail said, and I realized both that John had his hand up and that Gail knew his name. To be on such personal terms with a real author made something flutter in my heart, some dream I'd had in elementary school. But the more grounded voice in me said: *You've infiltrated their ranks, but you're a sheep in wolf's clothing.* It was right, of course. All the authors who were so impressed with our store and our idealism didn't know we were just a family of homeless bums.

"Would you hike the Pacific Crest Trail again?" John asked. It was pretty typical of him-- always wondering about regret.

"Absolutely!" Gail said in her lilting, child-like voice. She was 54 when she had hiked the Pacific Crest Trail and it had almost killed her; and she was 63 now. Even at 54, she was about twenty years older than most of the other hikers. I imagined she had experienced a lot of the discrimination we had experienced at our bookstore, but in reverse: Surely there were people who hadn't taken her seriously because she was too old to hike the Pacific Crest Trail.

"Absolutely," Gail said again. "In a heartbeat. No doubt about it. It was the best experience of my life. Nothing else was like that. I had never before had the experience-- and most people never do-- of relying only on myself for survival."

As soon as Gail indicated that she was done answering questions, the crowd stood up, most rushing to the back of the store to grab a book. Along with Anne, Gail's friend in the audience, I helped her out of her sandwich-board book-cover costume so that she could sit to sign books. While John rang up our customers' purchases, I started working to remove the extra chairs from the shop. I was afraid that by doing so, I might encourage customers to leave, but I was also afraid that with no room to mill about, people might not buy any books. While I was moving chairs, the elderly woman must have introduced herself to Porter, because I heard him exclaim "Really?" and collect her in a prim sort of embrace.

The woman named Anne and her teenaged daughter wandered about the store, picking up a copy of Gail's memoir, as well as an anthology put out by the Longmont Writer's Club.

"Tell her why you picked out this one," Anne said to her daughter, motioning at me.

"I'm in it," the girl said, grinning proudly to reveal straight white teeth. She wanted to impress a respected bookstore owner; I wondered what she would say to me if I was a homeless bag lady on the bus instead.

"Oh, wow! Congratulations! How cool to be in your first book in high school," I said, and I really meant it. I thought it was great. I was glad that writing was still acclaimed as a prestigious talent in schools. I wondered, though, out of the nine students who had been selected for the anthology, how many of them had mothers as wealthy and well-dressed as Anne.

Still clutching the book, the girl headed towards the counter. I hoped John would be as genuinely excited for her. For a while, we had been working with an organization in Boulder to teach a creative writing class to a group of at-risk and addicted youth, then teach them submission and self-publishing skills and help them publish an anthology of their work. Unfortunately, the funding had fallen through and the class never materialized. I hoped that resentment wouldn't color our opinions of the more privileged students who had managed to get themselves into an anthology. Telling the truth and making it interesting enough for other people to read was still hard work, no matter how many advantages one had in life.

John was conversing with a pair of interested old ladies, giving them the elevator speech about how buying from local stores benefited our community's economy. They nodded and smiled, but I knew they'd buy their groceries from Wal-Mart and Target when he was done.

After all the customers had their copies of Gail's memoir signed-- we sold nine, a new record for us-- John wrote Gail a check and I presented her and her husband with their Toblorone bars.

"Oh my goodness, thank you!" Gail exclaimed, wrapping me in an awkward embrace. "I've never had a bookstore owner give me chocolate before!"

Porter grinned as he pocketed his, and I felt satisfied that he felt just as strongly about Toblerones as my father did.

"I had a moment of worry, like, when I was setting out refreshments," I said, attempting to make conversation. "Since you're always eating one in the book, I thought Toblerones would be perfect for sort of themed refreshments, and then while I was setting them out, I thought, "Oh my gosh, what if she's sick of them now?'"

"No, no, it's perfect!" Gail exclaimed again, and John presented her with a check for seventy dollars.

"How much did we make?" I asked John after Gail and Porter left.

"Not as much as we gave her," John said, but I was still happy. Profit was profit, even if someone else had more.

One wild-haired man stayed behind after most of the audience had left; he wore a leather cowboy hat and was deeply tanned. His goatee was salt-and-peppered like his hair.

"So, you guys take, like, local books?" he asked with just a hint of disdain.

"Of course!" John and I said enthusiastically.

"I've got a couple I don't know if you'd be interested in," he said, inspecting his nails as if communicating with us was only an after-thought. This was common and we weren't offended; Pretending not to care protected the author just in case we were repulsed by the very idea that they had completed a book, which seemed to be what many authors thought our reaction would be.

This made me sad, because so many authors couldn't coincidentally share this paranoia for totally unrelated reasons; their hobby had obviously been met with disdain before. It was the only way to explain an entire class of people who were positively ashamed that they had put forth the effort to write fifty-thousand words about a single topic.

We gave the man a copy of our consignment contract, and after a short conversation about a Creative Writing class he taught at the local community college, he left us to stare at our empty and disheveled store and grin at each other in awe of our success.

"I didn't know that many people could fit in our store," I said.

"Me either," John replied. We went home and went to bed.

Six

Saturday, our libertarian friend Sam came up from Commerce City again on the bus. I don't know for sure that he was a libertarian, but he told John once that he enjoyed Ayn Rand's *Atlas Shrugged*, so I could only assume as much. He had come to Colorado much like John and I: on a whim. He and his cousins had packed up their belongings and had driven around the Rockies in a jeep, camping at night till they found an apartment. It took them two weeks. It had taken John and the kids and I almost four, and a hefty proportion of the several thousand dollars we had saved up for our prospective move.

But although Sam's cousins had found jobs, he was unemployed after a freelance design job had fallen through, and hadn't been able to help with rent for several months. He had till June 1st to come up with seven hundred dollars (his share of the rent), or he would need to move out. Too proud, like us, to go back to his home state and admit defeat, Sam was preparing for homelessness. He thought he'd have better luck in Longmont or Fort Collins than he had in Denver, and an old friend in Loveland didn't have room to house him but had room for some of Sam's belongings. The problem was that Sam didn't own a vehicle and had no way to get his belongings from Commerce City to Loveland. Well, we had a truck. It just didn't run. That's why Sam was here.

"I don't want you to fix our truck for nothing," I said. "And you know we can't pay you." Sam was an avid reader of my blog.

"It's not for nothing," Sam said. "I don't have any way to

keep my shit if I can't get your truck running."

So Sam came up on the bus from Commerce City to take a look at the truck. To be completely accurate, the truck *did* run, thanks to the new power steering belt, but it did not stop, and with the terrible metal-on-metal sound, continuing to drive it might render the truck unfixable. But's it's easier to say it doesn't run than to explain all that. That's what I call "accuracy tempered by brevity." Like calling John my husband. Or Lyric my step-son. It's easier than explaining we've been together for so long that 'boyfriend' seems too informal, and that we filed taxes together so we're pretty much common-law anyway. We're a family and we don't like to have to qualify it with various attributes. Plus, we knew authors wouldn't take us as seriously as business owners if we referred to each other as boyfriend and girlfriend. Like we're dating now but might break up next week, or something. So in front of customers or to the newspaper, John always called me his wife and I called him my husband. At parties and around our peers, back when we lived in Wichita and still had peers, he still called me his girlfriend, though.

Sam came by the shop about eleven; he'd gotten off the bus up the block from our shop, and he was carrying a camping pack and a toolbox. The camping pack had a grill in it; he'd offered to bring it up so we could cook. We had some bratwursts in our fridge in the backroom, courtesy of the food pantry, but no way to cook them. Raw meat doesn't do so good in the microwave.

We all chatted at the shop for a bit before John and Sam left to take a bus back to the Wal-Mart parking lot, where our truck rested, a parking space between it and our motorhome. I stayed with the kids to keep the shop open a little later, but the bus stopped running that far north at six thirty, so we couldn't stay till our usual closing time of eight o'clock unless we wanted to walk back to Wal-Mart. So we closed the shop early to catch the bus, even though no one came to the shop at all between when Sam and John left with the camping pack and toolbox, and when I left with the kids and the bratwurst.

Sophie and Lyric and I waited against a young elm tree planted in a rounder in the sidewalk, because the bench seat was occupied. This stop was not a true bus stop with a seat under an awning, but just a metal sign indicating the stop and a sidewalk bench that sat nearby, as if by happenstance. Sophie played with rollie-pollies until the 324 came; it was the same bus driver as the southbound 324 we had taken from Wal-Mart to the shop that morning. He recognized us; it was hard for people not to recognize Sophie and Lyric. I wondered how many bus drivers recognized us, wondering why we left Wal-Mart every morning and went back every night. Once, we got in a taxi at the shop, later in the evening after the bus had stopped running, only to realize it was a taxi driver who had dropped us off at Wal-Mart a week prior. He did recognize us. A neighbor who got off work late at Wal-Mart would give us a ride home, John explained. Cheaper than taking a taxi up into the mountains. When we hopped out of the taxi, Sophie pointedly proclaimed, "Time to go shopping for groceries at Wal-Mart, now!" as she headed towards the front doors. She was learning, too young, how to keep a secret.

"We aren't going to the house on wheels to sleep?" Lyric asked, confused by Sophie's acting. John rolled his eyes in exasperation at our cover being blown yet again, and put his hand roughly on Lyric's shoulder to steer him towards the Wal-Mart entrance. It wasn't that Lyric was solidly against lying; For example: Yes, he had stayed in time-out while I went to the bathroom. No, he had not touched my nail polish. No, that was not nail polish on his face. Or his pants. Or the chair. And certainly not on his nails.

No, Lyric's problem was not an unwillingness to lie; simply a complete, and totally age-appropriate, ignorance of the reasons for our lies. When it suited him, he was happy to lie. He was just really, really bad at it.

Sophie, on the other hand, understood too much.

I didn't say anything to the driver of the northbound 324, opting instead to take the children to the back of the bus and hope they stayed quiet. On our ride to Wal-Mart, I discovered that Sophie had a stowaway, and I tossed the incumbent rollie-pollie out the open window. At the main bus terminal at on Coffman, by Roosevelt Park and the rec center, the bus driver stopped the bus and got off to take a break while he waited for passengers, and Lyric whined that there wasn't any air. He was echoing a complaint he'd heard from a passenger on a previous trip at this stop when the driver turned off the bus and also the air conditioning.

"The windows are open," I told him. "There wasn't any air conditioning *on*. There's just as much air as there was before."

As we neared Wal-Mart, everyone else got off the bus, leaving only me and my children for the final stop.

"Is there somewhere more convenient I can drop you off?" the driver asked in a nonchalant way meant to be kind. He looked at me through the rear-view mirror that must be meant for spying on passengers, for no driver could be expected to see the rear window past all the passengers who might stand in the aisle.

"Nah, the regular bus stop is fine," I said. "We just got a broken-down truck in the parking lot." Which was true, and conveniently explained our situation.

As the children and I approached, I saw that the hood of the truck was up, and John was leaning against it, drinking a bottle of craft beer. Sam was sitting, next to the children's car seats, on the open tailgate with another beer. They had two six-packs; one from Breckinridge Brewing and one from Left Hand Brewing. I wondered who paid and where they'd stopped; they didn't sell craft beer at Wal-Mart. I hoped they didn't plan on finishing it off, because if they did, John would probably then go into Wal-Mart and get caught stealing really cheap beer-- or worse, spend money on it. He was alright with a beer or two, but if he drank more than that, he usually didn't stop. It wasn't unusual for him to drink a couple of six-packs a day.

"I sure hope this fixes it," John said, holding up a square box nearly a foot long and wide and six inches deep. "Or else I bought this for nothing."

I pretended to be unfazed, rather than asking how much it, whatever it was, cost.

"We need to be able to lift the truck off the ground," John said, explaining the situation.

"We can lift the truck up off the ground with the jack that came with it, but we need something to set it up on," Sam said. I realized that children's car-seats were in the bed of the truck because the jack had been under the back seat of the truck.

The men consulted with each other while I found a pen and some scrap paper to occupy the children. I wondered if John and Sam had been waiting for some kind of input for me, or if I simply happened to arrive while they were taking a break after reaching a stopping point.

"We're gonna go steal some cinderblocks," Sam announced, walking towards me.

"Steal-steal them?" I asked. Not because I was concerned, but more curious whether he meant discarded remnants from construction, or actual stocked products with a SKU code and everything. Either could be possible.

"Not steal-steal. Borrow," John interjected. "They're just over in the garden section, outside in the parking lot. We're going to put them back when we're done."

I almost thought that might be more risky than just taking them, but I didn't object. Sam and John wandered off to collect a shopping cart for their project, and I attended to the children. Much quicker than I expected, Sam and John returned with the shopping cart, loaded down with a couple of cinder blocks.

"There's some just over there!" Sam said excitedly, pointing to the edge of the parking lot. He and John unloaded the cart next to the truck.

"How many more do we need?" John asked. Sam stacked the blocks up, a little wobblier than I was comfortable with, to measure them against the wheel of the truck.

"Four," Sam said resolutely. John took the shopping cart and headed towards the sandy lot behind the propane kiosk between the west edge of our alcove and Main Street, which was actually Highway 287 north of Wal-Mart. He returned with more cinder blocks, and I left our tiny motorhome for the behemoth of Wal-Mart to get a sandwich for everyone for dinner.

The sandwiches cost two dollars each, and I got everyone a nectarine, too, which cost three dollars total, and two bottles of Gatorade for eighty cents each. Our recently-approved food stamps came to about $550 a month, which meant $17 a day for a family of four, or $1.48 per person per meal, which we also had to spend on any clean water we wanted. Saturday's dinner came to far over our per-meal per-person allowance, but we had just gotten them and were so excited at the prospect of real food, or at least some semblance to it, that we weren't rationing ourselves very strictly yet. Also we were feeding Sam, but he was fixing our truck for us so I was okay with that.

"This close!" Sam shouted at me, holding up his thumb and forefinger as I returned with the sandwiches.

"We don't have the right size wrench to get the bolts off," John explained, and I pretended that he had indeed explained everything and I understood perfectly that it was truly a travesty. I made the children go sit on their beds inside the motorhome and gave them their sandwiches, while John and Sam stumbled about like zombies, smart-phones held in front of their bodies like divining rods, trying to pick up a wifi signal. None of us had paid a phone bill in months, so we couldn't use the allowance of gigabytes that comes with a phone plan, and instead we relied on using the smart phones like a laptop: only to pick up free wifi wherever we found it.

The Super 8 across the street had wifi, which John had used to download *Who Framed Roger Rabbit?* once, but neither John nor Sam felt like going to the effort to cross Highway 66 in the evening rush-hour traffic. I went back inside to check on the children.

"I don't like my sandwich. It has leafs," Lyric said, mispronouncing the plural and picking at some greens that looked as if the sandwich technician might have mixed up the iceberg lettuce and the spinach.

"Eat it anyway," I said. It was probably the first vegetable he'd actually been presented with in months. Prior to our homelessness, I was real big on home-cooked meals, and not the meat-and-potatoes variety. However, my constant schemes to get the children to eat a serving of vegetables a day were met with extreme resistance on Lyric's end, usually in the form of gagging; or, if his bluff was called, vomiting. John had taken to forcing Lyric to eat his vegetables, whether he puked them up or not; It was sort of borderline child abuse, but we were stuck between a rock and a hard place. Giving in to Lyric's demands when he made himself puke would only reinforce that his method had worked. However, with prepacked, unheated food from the food pantry as our only source of nutrition in the two months between when we became homeless and were approved for food stamps, Lyric hadn't seen a fresh green leaf in months. I naively hoped he'd humor me.

I peeked out the window. John was conversing with a Latino man in a red Ford Explorer that was parked a little south of us in the alcove. I stepped outside to make sure Sam had enough Gatorade.

"He's going to take us to AutoZone before they close so we can get a wrench. We have to hurry, we have like ten minutes," John said, and he and Sam raced for the Explorer before I could remind John to actually eat his sandwich.

I stepped back inside the motorhome to wait, and found a puke-covered Lyric. I ran back outside.

"John, Lyric threw up everywhere!" I shouted as the Explorer pulled around the alcove.

"I'm sorry, I'll take care of it when I get back!" John shouted back, leaning out the window as the Explorer sped away.

I stepped back inside the motorhome.

"You little shit," I said to Lyric, who was waiting quietly to see whether or not he'd get a spanking. If he were really and truly sick, he'd be bawling. It was sort of funny how being unexpectedly sick upset Lyric so much, when he so routinely made himself vomit on purpose if he didn't like what I served for dinner. I guess he just didn't like to puke if he wasn't intending to. Which was pretty normal, I guess, but most kids didn't intentionally puke so very *often.*

"You still have to eat your sandwich, you know," I told him, trying to maintain some semblance of consistency with our former life.

I moved Lyric outside to eat on the asphalt, and cleaned up most of the vomit with Wal-Mart receipts because I didn't have any napkins and those aren't covered by food stamps. I gave the kids each a nectarine after they finished their sandwiches, which I thought was being pretty generous in Lyric's case, and I gave Sophie an old date book I'd stopped using and the Uniball pen I carried religiously. Sophie drew people in the date book, and Lyric sat on the asphalt, and I typed away on my laptop in between chasing Rigby away from licking sticky vomit off of Lyric.

John and Sam returned in the Explorer a little after dusk, though the fluorescent parking lot lights made it hard to tell. John immediately snatched up his sandwich, angry that he had forgotten it.

"Oh, and pack a bowl for Red SUV guy. We promised him a bowl for driving us. He didn't want to drive with no insurance. I don't know what he's so worried about, I've *never* driven with insurance."

This was a slight exaggeration; he'd had insurance, like, twice, when he bought a week's worth in order to show proof when he purchased tags. I sent the children inside, telling them to lay down for bed. I wasn't mad about having to pack a bowl for the stranger, because there was already half-smoked bowl in the pipe, and it would be rude to compensate for the ride with a bowl that was already half-smoked. This left me no option but to smoke the half-bowl by myself, which is why I didn't object at all.

After I loaded a new bowl and handed it off to the long-haired Explorer guy, John and Sam discovered that they still were in need of some part or other. A hex wrench, I think they said. They decided to go in to Wal-Mart to steal it.

"I don't believe in stealing," Sam said, "but only from other *people*. Wal-Mart doesn't count."

"Exactly," John said. "I'll spend money at local stores. I would never steal from a mom-and-pop store. I know they're trying to make ends meet, like us. But Wal-Mart is different."

"Kinda weird that we're so anti-Wal-Mart but we're living off of them."

"No, no, fuck that. We're *living off* of them. We're not supporting them," John said. "We've bought a bottle of water from Wal-Mart, like, once?" He looked at me and I nodded. He was right; we had to be in really dire straights to consider spending money at Wal-Mart. When we first moved to Longmont, we spent thirty dollars on a bath rug at Ace Hardware to avoid going to Wal-Mart. And even Ace Hardware was a chain, but we hadn't showered since leaving our home in Wichita before my laser aberration surgery, and for some reason a bath mat seemed necessary for taking a shower, and we looked in about twelve different local shops before deciding that we weren't totally opposed to Ace Hardware's business practices. They sold a lot of locally-produced tools and kitchen utensils, after all, and allowed dogs in the store.

"We don't *support* Wal-Mart," John reiterated. "America has been supporting them for long enough. Let *them* support *us* for a while. They're paying our fucking rent. We've lived in the parking lot for a month now. That would have cost, like, four hundred dollars at an RV camp. Fuck, we get free rent from Wal-Mart. We steal everything we get from Wal-Mart. That's not supporting them. *They're* supporting *us*. And I don't feel a damn bit bad about it. We're homeless because of what Wal-Mart did to the economy. Everything's Big-Box retailers now, even books. Business owners can't make a living. Everyone kept saying, oh, the economy will improve and jobs will come back. Fuck that. They've been saying that since 2001. Fuck that. I was like ten years old in 2001. The last time there were 'jobs,' by these people's estimation, I was nine years old. I didn't fucking work then. I was nine. I've never fucking worked in an economy that had 'jobs.' So people keep saying, oh, the jobs will come back, the economy will improve, and I just don't fucking believe them. I'm not going to sit around on my ass waiting for jobs that I really don't believe in. They're liking fucking unicorns, man. An economy with 'jobs' available, *real* jobs where you can make a living, it's a fucking myth. It hasn't existed since our parents were our age. And they want us to sit around and work our asses off in unpaid internships, waiting for these mythological jobs to come back. It's like waiting for the Second Coming. I'm not going to work for nothing while I wait for Jesus to come back with his jobs, and reward all of us who have been faithful and worked for nothing while we waited. Fuck that. I'm a fucking atheist. I'm going to make my own job."

"Right on," the long-haired Explorer guy said, handing me back the pipe while he contemplated John's message of an atheistic economy.

"So I make my own fucking job, right? That's a responsible thing to do. I work my ass off. You know that, right?"

"You do," I said. "Sixty hour weeks, every week, for, what, six months now?"

"And what's it gotten us?" John asked. "Shit. Wal-Mart stepped in while everyone was starving, waiting for their precious jobs to come back, and people were so excited about cheap food and minimum-wage jobs that they forgot all about Main Street. No one buys anything from a grocer they know by name any more. Even if we wanted to, to support the little guy or whatever, there's none left. Wal-Mart killed 'em. Killed their jobs. And they'll get ours, too, before too long. Fuck, people can buy books at Wal-Mart. We're not just competing with Amazon and Barnes and Noble. We're competing with fucking Wal-Mart. How the fuck are we supposed to compete with Wal-Mart?"

"You sabotage them?" Sam suggested, grinning. John laughed.

"I'm not sabotaging them. They know people shoplift. They account for it. It doesn't hurt their profits one iota. But they can take care of some of my bills for a while. They can take care of my rent. My groceries. My truck." He kicked his Chevy, which wobbled dangerously on its cinderblocks. "Fuck that. I'm getting a hex wrench." And John and Sam began the trek across the parking lot, leaving me to write a well-intentioned book in the moonlight and parking-lot lights, a book that would never see a Wal-Mart shelf, because big publishers had done to writing jobs exactly what Wal-Mart had done to mom-and-pop grocery jobs.

"Fuck jobs," I could imagine Kerouac saying. Whiskey costs money, but Kerouac had his G.I. Bill. I had student loans and weed.

"This is the hardest thing I've ever stolen," John said upon returning to the RV, removing a two-inch metal cylinder from his pocket. I stared down at him from the top bunk above the cab. "I had to break this black plastic stuff. Whatever."

The men went to go do whatever it is you do with this two-inch metal cylinder, and then suddenly John howled and Sam laughed raucously. I climbed down from the bunk and peered out the screen door. Sam was playfully punching John in the arm, repeatedly, and John's face was in his hands as he walked in circles, Sam twisting around to keep punching him.

"He got the same size we already have," Sam explained as I stepped out of the motorhome.

"I thought it was bigger!" John cried. "I thought it was a size bigger! I got the biggest one they had!" Sam punched him again.

"What can you do?" I asked.

"We can't go back right after leaving..." John moaned.

"Would you like me to go?" I asked. John looked up at me from his hands.

"Do you think you could?"

I wasn't nervous about shoplifting, but I was nervous about getting the right thing. I've never understood parts, of anything, really. Not just cars and trucks and tool boxes. Telephones. Toasters. My laptop, with the number keys that mysteriously stopped working. Lamps. I didn't really understand anything.

Except, ironically, the human body. Big stuff, kidneys and arteries. Little stuff, hormones and parasites and neurotransmitters. While John shared my affinity for pharmaceuticals, their workings-- biochemistry, or just biology in general-- were really the one mechanical thing that he had no interest in or understanding of whatsoever. I tried to explain antioxidants in terms of getting an oil change, once, but that basically ended with me being told that I obviously didn't understand the purpose behind or workings of an oil change.

"Yeah, I can get it," I said firmly. "Now, what is it again?" I tried that last part as nonchalantly as possible, as if I knew exactly what it was I was supposed to obtain but some trivial other piece of information, maybe the brand name, had happened to slip my mind. John, gratefully, went along with this.

"It's a hex wrench," he said. "Get one larger than three-eighths of an inch." I figured that must be the diameter of the cylinder.

"Is it in the car section or the tool section?" I asked, cringing at my own ignorance. John, thankfully, again chose to ignore it rather than calling it out.

"The tool section. But don't walk around the garden section to steal it, because that's what we did."

I wanted to ask whether "larger than three-eighths of an inch" meant "at least three-eighths of an inch, or larger," or whether three-eighths was too small. But I was afraid to ask any more questions-- John's patience with humoring me was probably wearing thin-- so I donned my big brown-and-pink baja hoodie, which came down to my knees and had a front pocket large enough to carry a cat in, and retrieved my large leather purse from the RV. I trekked into Wal-Mart, looking sort of like I was ready to ride a burro down the Grand Canyon, and began my search for the tool section.

There were a lot of empty spaces in the row of wrenches in the tool department, which worried me. I found some labeled 'Hex Wrench' and 'Hex Wrench Conversion' and 'Hex Socket' and other variations that didn't mean much to me. They were little cylinders with a hexagonal hole on one end and a square on the other, or a hexagon sticking out, or a cube sticking out, or some other combination. I found a set of three, with one missing, and I wondered if it was the one John had stolen; but, it seemed from the packaging that the missing piece was a half-inch, so that couldn't be right. Maybe someone else was stealing hex wrenches, too. I found a set of about fifteen cylinders, in a all different sixes, from a sixteenth of an inch up to two inches. The set was in black plastic, about a foot long, and as John had insinuated, the plastic was going to be really hard to break. So I carried the set with me, down the Home aisle, arms at my sides. My huge baja hoodie hung around me, the sleeves a good five inches longer than my arms. The set was mostly covered by my sleeves, anyway, so it wasn't hard to put the whole set up the baggy sleeve of my hoodie. I walked like this to the grocery aisles, where I picked out two more bottles of Gatorade and a bag of chocolate-covered coffee beans, and while digging through my purse for the food-stamp card, I transferred the set from my sleeve to the inside of my purse.

I scanned my Gatorade and candy at the self-checkout kiosk and headed out the door, and the detectors at the door went wild, beeping as I passed through them. I shot them an angry glare, visibly annoyed, and continued on. I found that looking annoyed, rather than scared, was key to getting away with shoplifting. No one questioned you if you acted entitled.

At the conclusion of my trek back across the parking lot, I presented John and Sam with my prize. Their glee at the large package quickly turned to disappointment.

"It's the wrong part," Sam said. "This is, like, the opposite end of the hex wrench that we need. These are sockets. Male and female parts."

"It will still be useful, though," John quickly assured me. "For other stuff."

"God dammit," I said. "I don't think they had the right

thing, then. This was the only thing larger than three-eighths of an inch that said 'hex wrench' on it."

"I told you," John said. "The reason I didn't get one big enough is because there *wasn't* one."

"I think they're out of stock," I said. "There were a lot of empty spaces."

"This will still be useful, though," John said, holding the wrench set. "For other stuff. It will be really nice to have."

"We just need to figure out a way to get that bolt off," Sam said.

But we couldn't think of anything else to try that night, so we smoked another bowl and went to bed.

Sam slept up in the top bunk, above the dashboard (I had surreptitiously removed all of our sex toys from our bed and hid them in a plastic bag in a cabinet, while John and Sam were occupied with the truck), and John and I slept on the spare mattress on the floor of the RV, between Sophie's bed and Lyric's. We cradled each other close and whispered promises to each other about what type of home we'd live in some day.

"People just aren't meant to live like this," John said, staring at the ceiling. "They're just not."

I looked around at our filthy motorhome, with plastic bags taped around the holes in the ceiling, the wasp nest on the window, the useless sink and oven and refrigerator, lights that would never turn on, outlets that didn't work, the hulking air conditioning unit and heater that were worthless without electricity. I thought of the filthy sink and toilet and shower in the bathroom, the water that didn't run.

"People have lived without electricity or plumbing for thousands of years," I said stiffly, defensively. "We can survive without a fridge or shower."

John turned on his side to look at me. "No," he said. "I meant the fluorescent lights."

Somehow it hadn't occurred to me that it was as bright as day in the Wal-Mart parking lot. While working on the truck, it had been a benefit, but John was right. People weren't meant to live under constant light. That gave me something to think about, so I lay in John's arms and listened to the chatter of confused birds, their circadian rhythms totally fucked.

Seven

The next day was Sunday; not quite Memorial Day, but still Memorial Day Weekend, and there was a festive air amongst the residents of the Wal-Mart parking lot. This was because the population had doubled overnight with campers who were not homeless, but simply parking their RV at Wal-Mart so they wouldn't have to pay for a camp spot before heading to the lake. Probably Lake Carter, just up Highway 287, which was Main Street in town. Lake Carter was where John and the kids and I camped, mostly, whenever we came down from the mountains during our pilgrimage the previous summer.

While we were in the mountains, we had a couple regular spots: Longs Peak, though it was oft overcrowded with serious athletes who began the trek up the fourteener at three in the morning. However, this meant that it was quieter, less rowdy than most summer campsites. Our favorite spot was in Cold Springs, where one particular campsite was blessed with several alcoves made up of umbrella-like pine trees, the spaces under the trees tall enough to stand in and hidden from view of other campers by the thick evergreen branches. We used one as a kitchen, where John cooked with an illegal camp stove (illegal because of the wild fires), and in the privacy under another tree, John and I fucked on the brown pine needles while the kids slept in the tent, which was set up under a third tree, a little ways away. I think this was what John liked best about that spot.

We also had a spot between Grand Lake and Granby, on open land where camp sites weren't marked and moose lolled through the clearings of pine-tree stumps and past our tent at daybreak. At Hermit Mountain, outside Estes Park, we camped on a granite outcropping, and drove down the mountain, speeding around switch-backs so fast I was scared we'd drive off the edge, when Sophie tripped while playing outside our tent and busted open her head on a granite boulder. She got two stitches in Estes Park, where the prompt medical attention without regard to our financial situation cemented my opinion of Progressive Colorado.

By far our least favorite campsite was at Robber's Roost, which wasn't such a bad campsite as it was high in elevation. While making our way up to the peak of the Continental Divide in the south, at a pass near Golden, we realized that nightfall would approach before we made it to the west side of the mountain, and we needed to stop and set up camp. Night fell all the more quickly due to the fact that we were three-quarters of the way up the very steep eastern slope of the mountain. It was also at Robber's Roost that a pole in our tent broke, and John tended to that rather than starting a fire, while I was instructed to dig through our forty-gallon ice chest for the fish he would grill for dinner.

My hands were in eight inches of ice water for twenty minutes while I dug through our frozen supplies in the dark. I cried and cried, but couldn't give up till I found the fish. By that time, the sun was well gone and the high-altitude temperature had dropped. My hands were so stiff I couldn't help at all with the tent repairs, which frustrated John, and no matter how close I got to the fire, my hands simply would not warm up again. John cooked fish and potatoes in the dark, and it was only the next day, when we saw the remaining potatoes in daylight, that we realized our potatoes had been full of maggots. I think that was the highest elevation we ever slept at, and it's the coldest I ever was at night. Before we were homeless, anyway.

But when we gave up on finding affordable rent in the mountains, and had inspired ourselves with plenty of picnics along rocky vistas, we came down from the mountains and camped at Lake Carter while we scoured the area for affordable flat-land apartments. That's how we wound up in Longmont anyhow. Lake Carter was a dammed lake, artificial, with brilliant red rocks all the way around and a man-made red beach and a marina with sailboating and motor-boating and all kinds of activities for people who owned big motorized recreational vehicles they called 'toys.' A lot of people came to Lake Carter for Memorial Day. It's super-American to 'go to the lake' on a holiday. But if you camped at Wal-Mart, you didn't have to pay for a campsite. There is a certain class of people who can afford to 'go to the lake' for Memorial Day, yet park their RV at Wal-Mart instead, and the more permanent residents of the Wal-Mart parking lot fit right in with the newcomers and didn't stick out at all. Most assumed we were fellow vacationers who had simply arrived a little earlier. In that, perhaps there is a certain distinction between 'vacationer' and 'traveler.'

With all the people milling about, walking to Wal-Mart and returning with sun-tan lotion and potato salad, there was a certain air of excitement, which I think we all caught. They were excited to get to the lake. We were excited to get the truck fixed. We were excited to eat sausages, left out overnight then grilled on a George Foreman. We were excited to blend in as fellow Normal People and not as Homeless People.

I'm not sure why Sam brought the George Foreman grill. I guess something just didn't click. He knew our motorhome had no electricity. He knew the grill needed to be plugged in. Somehow, it just didn't quite click.

There was a propane refill center between our alcove and the highway, and their small office-shack had an outlet on the back wall. John had discovered this while snooping around looking for cement blocks. The propane kiosk was closed on Sundays, and John figured we'd cook our Memorial Day bratwursts over there. I wondered if there were special fines for trespassing and cooking with a potentially flammable appliance next to a giant propane tank. I know George Foremans aren't the most dangerous appliance out there, but in my incapable hands, any cooking utensil can be deadly.

More pressing matters arose: How to remove a stripped bolt without the hex wrench we lacked.

I can offer no clues as to how the stripped-ness and hex-ness were related, only report what John and Sam indicated was the problem.

"Do you think you could find, like, a really wide rubber band?" John asked.

"Like this," Sam said, holding his forefinger and thumb an inch a part.

"Do you think the kind they use to hold vegetables together will work?" I asked.

"Maybe."

"I could buy some leeks with food stamps and then I wouldn't even have to steal the rubber band."

"I don't know if it will be, like, wide enough. It's gotta be wide enough for the bolt to sit in it."

"I'll try," I said. I offered to bring the children inside to take them to use the restroom and get breakfast while I searched for a wide rubber band. John and Sam had simply peed in the toilet, which I guess wasn't super unsanitary because the toilet bowl did flush and the septic tank was fine, but with no electric-powered water pump, there was no way to rinse the toilet or wash their hands.

With the promise of donuts for children who behaved, I took the kids down the office supplies aisle first, after using the restroom and washing both their dirty faces, Lyric's cheek crusted with vomit I hadn't been able to clean off with receipts. In the office supply aisle, the only abnormally-sized rubber bands were the extra thin ones. A plastic bag of standard-width rubber bands had a gaping hole in the center; someone else had needed only one rubber band as well. I pretended to inspect the hole and removed another rubber band, and wondered how many shoplifters would benefit from the first's rip-work before the package was discovered and thrown away by the stop-loss department.

I tried the tool section, again, just for good measure, but the Hex Wrench stock space was still full of empty shelves. I got a role of electric tape, because I'd earlier overheard Sam mention that he'd forgot his, and I wanted to pre-empt an additional trip to Wal-Mart, as multiple trips in a day made me nervous about getting caught. I figured the average shift was about eight hours, and I didn't want to be seen by the same employee multiple times in one shift.

After the tool section, I traversed the width of Wal-Mart, toddlers in tow like effervescent goldfish, bouncing back and forth as displays on the opposite sides of the aisles captivated their attention. I herded them onwards with donut promises. In the produce section, I also let them pick out their heart's desire (a plastic bowl of pre-cut watermelon) and I inspected a bunch of leeks with a critical eye, removing the extra-wide rubber band to turn each leek over and examine the backs for crushed spots and bruises. Unsatisfied that this bunch of leeks met my stringent requirements, I replaced the bunch on the shelf with an indignant sniff, pocketing the rubber band. An innocent mistake.

We paid for our watermelon and donuts with the food-stamp card, and crossed the parking lot again to the land of motorhomes. I set the children up on the steps to the motorhome, our white-trash equivalent of a front porch, and presented the men with my rubber bands.

"Too small," Sam said, throwing the standard sized rubber band into the bed of the truck. "Might work." He held up the wide purple band from the leeks, inspecting it with a critical eye, then working it into a wrench.

"I also got some electrical tape, just in case," I said, digging through my purse. Both men exhaled excitedly.

"Your clairvoyance skills are improving," John said. "We were just talking about how we might try electrical tape if this doesn't work."

I was very pleased with myself for my foresight, but within eight minutes (the approximate time it takes a four-year-old to consume a large donut and lick his fingers clean), I was cursing myself for not stealing a box of chalk, too. Hard-pressed to find entertainment for the children, I headed for the median between our alcove and the Panda Express parking lot, and collected about ten fist-sized rocks from the median.

"Here," I said, giving them to the children. "Let's make pictures."

Making bas-relief images of people from rocks on the ground proved a successful source of entertainment, and the children made other images, too: a sun, a house, a dog. I brought them more rocks and let them take turns trading rocks for the especially sparkly or unusually-colored ones. We used the previous night's nectarine pits as eyes.

"We got it!" Sam said, walking over to me and the kids, holding something small and covered in grease high in the air like a trophy. I couldn't tell exactly what it was, because both the object and Sam's hand were completely black. "This is what I love about cars! When you actually *get* something!"

John was crouched next to the front wheel, his hands similarly covered in black substance, holding what looked like a small wire.

"Are we gonna drain this stuff?" John asked Sam.

"Nah, I don't think we have any way to flush it. Just try to keep any more from spilling out. I'll get the new brake pad." Then to me he turned and said, "It's gonna be done before too long. Why don't you go start the brats?"

The children were entertained with their rocks, so I set off to start grilling the bratwursts for lunch. John had already located the outlet at the propane shack kiosk building. He had plugged in the George Foreman, so it was heating up, and my only job would to be to find the location of the grill and cook the meat. He made it sound like he'd already done all the hard work.

Stepping over the sagging barbed-wire fence between the asphalt Wal-Mart parking lot and the dry, sand-blown desert of the propane station parking lot, I felt like I was on a hot, dusty stage, for all the drivers on Highway 287 to see. Luckily, the George Foreman grill was both easy to locate and hidden from the view of both highways by the shack and an adjacent trash dumpster. I crouched on the ground and opened the grill, wondering how to begin. In addition to the package of turkey bratwursts from the food pantry, John had bought a package of hot dogs, a bag of hot dog buns, and a bag of fancy Sara Lee rolls I assumed were meant for the bratwursts. When John said that we had never bought more than a water bottle from Wal-Mart, he was speaking the truth, if he meant our own money. But with food stamps and no independent grocery stores-- and our close proximity to the corporate giant-- we got plenty of food from Wal-Mart, whether we paid for it or not (we didn't). As far as I was concerned, food stamps were little more than a government subsidy of Wal-Mart and Safeway.

It was a problem, but one to which I didn't see a solution: Limiting the amount of food stamps that could be spent at Big Box stores would only hurt the recipients that food stamps were intended to help. And where else could they be spent? Independent grocery stores were practically non-existent and Farmer's Markets had inflated prices, but the real problem was transportation. It was difficult enough for most poor people to scrape up enough for gas or a bus ticket to get to Wal-Mart, which in most cities seems to be on the bus line. In fact, I'd recently read that a staggering proportion of Americans live in a so-called food desert-- An area where no grocery stores are within walking distance or within walking distance of public transportation. This means that residents in these areas who do not own cars are forced to spend their food stamps at gas stations, where prices are inflated and fresh vegetables are completely absent from the limited options.

Sometimes, it's easy to forget how lucky you are.

I didn't have any silverware or dishes, so I opted to use hot dog buns as both. The bratwursts came in a little styrofoam tray that would have worked nicely as a serving tray, had it not been soaking in raw meat juice. So I carefully placed the bratwursts on the George Foreman, tossed the juicy tray in the dumpster next to me, and spread the hot dog buns out on top of their plastic bag, hoping that too much dust wouldn't get kicked up in the cooking process.

The bratwursts started to burn where they were in contact

with the grill, but the sides were still totally raw. I didn't have any forks or tongs to turn the bratwursts, so I used a hot dog bun, gripping the meat inside the bun and turning it, ever-fearful my finger tips would touch the grill. By the time I had turned all the brats twice, the hot dog bun was completely shredded, and I used another. Grease dripped from the grill onto the dusty ground, leaving dark-colored blobs in the light dirt that was so dry, it might actually have been comprised entirely of the finest and tiniest of sand particles. There was an impression of a racoon's forepaw in the dirt nearby, and I figured that some oversized rodent would probably enjoy the grease droppings and the shredded, half-toasted hot dog buns.

I returned to the RV with a Sara Lee bag of bratwursts and hot dogs nestled in what was left of the buns. Both men were completely black from the elbows-down, and were now on the passenger's side tire.

"We're done," John said, crouching by the tire and holding up a thin tube, as he been doing on the other side of the truck last time I saw him. "We just got to put the new brake pad on and lower the truck."

I went to give the children their hot dogs, and sure enough, John and Sam were soon finished. They washed their hands with stuff called Orange Soap, which smelled refreshing and contained lots of little pieces of pumice. The black came right off in a grey sort of foam, and they took turns pouring from one of our gallons of water to rinse the foam off. The Orange Soap seemed to work so well that when I was done eating, I sat on the tailgate of the truck and washed my feet with it. My feet had taken on the peculiar hue and form consistent with a life lived homeless, even after only two months. My soles were thick with callouses, which had black dirt ground deep into the cracks. Orange Soap took off all the dirt, and some of the skin and callouses, too. My feet didn't turn out their most attractive-- pieces of skin were obviously missing, giving them a sort of chapped look-- but they were a lot cleaner than they were before, and felt clean, too, and that made me happy.

The men were much more pleased with the bratwursts than they were with their clean hands, but most of all they were pleased that the truck had brakes. I was pleased, too. John was somewhat irate with me for giving the children hot dogs without ketchup or relish, and I was a little exasperated with him not only for thinking that would be a good idea, given that they had both torn their hot dogs in half and removed the meat from the buns but eaten nothing within two minutes of receiving their lunch, but also that he didn't trust my judgement, as if I hadn't predicted what they'd do to their hot dogs. But overall, the air was festive, even though all the vacationers had left the parking lot for greener pastures or greener lakes or whatever.

Left in the parking lot were a few motorhomes and lived-in vehicles; Axel seemed to have moved on, though his truck was still in the parking lot, and also there was the man and his wife who had asked if I was 'new'; a big white truck, newer than ours, where lived a girl from Texas and her boyfriend and their Catahoula (Rigby enjoyed the company of the Catahoula, though it was much younger and larger than her); an old camper-van in which lived a probably schizophrenic woman named Melissa and her four cats; a van with a mother, father, and their teenaged son; the maroon Explorer, whose owner had given John and Sam a ride to AutoZone; and a few odd cars and trucks with single occupants whom we hadn't met yet.

Melissa came over to talk, and we offered her a bratwurst, feeling truly All-American, like suburban neighbors who grill stuff with each other on Memorial Day, even though I'd grilled ours behind a dumpster. She took it and started talking about hemp in between ravenous bites.

"Have you read *The Emperor Wears No Clothes?*" she asked. Sam had, and they started discussing the Founding Fathers and their hemp use.

Melissa wore another uniform typical of the American Homeless: T-shirt advertising something, I think it was a brand of horse pick, but it was so far removed from Melissa as an individual that it just didn't matter. Bra with very little support.

Basketball shorts, which came past her knees. Tennis shoes and crew socks that were once white. Hard to tell how long since the socks had been washed, because the Wal-Mart parking lot was so dusty that your feet turned brown again less than a day after a shower. My own callouses were already taking on some dirt in the cracks, half an hour after being washed with Orange Soap.

Melissa seemed to like Sam, which was fortunate but unexpected. He wasn't quite homeless yet but seemed to believe he was 'one of them,' when even John and I were aware that we didn't quite fit the mores of the culture into which we had been thrust. Sam, for example, often said that he would be happy to sleep in his hammock, anywhere he could find to hang it up. Chris would have been annoyed at Sam for not trying to fit in, for sticking out without caring. And if the police chased Sam off for being too conspicuous with his camping, he could always swallow his pride and go back to Utah. Those who had no pride left didn't have that option; they could only try their best to fit in.

When I had gone to the free clinic at the homeless shelter for my foot, I listened as a nurse gave the red-haired man next to me tips on caring for his gout.

"Whenever you have a chance, take your shoes and socks off and let your feet dry out," the nurse had told him. "I don't care if you're just sitting at the smoking bench outside, take your shoes and socks off. When you stop for the night. You got to let your feet dry out as often as you can."

I wondered whether the man ever followed her advice, or if he was willing to risk his feet getting worse for the sake of blending in and not appearing to be homeless. It could mean the difference between getting to stay up all night inside Winchell's and being forced to stay the night outside in the snow.

Melissa was talking about pride.

"You have to drop all of it to be able to fly signs," she said. "If you have any pride left at all, take it out, put it in your pocket, save it for later, whatever. But it ain't gonna do you no good while you're flyin' signs."

To Sam, as well, flying signs was not rock-bottom but yet

another social experiment, like sleeping outdoors. When he and his cousins had first arrived in Colorado, they had paid a homeless man in Denver to fly signs for them. I have no idea how the arrangement came about, but supposedly Sam and his cousins gave the guy a ride to a "better spot" every day, bought him stuff, whatever, in exchange for a portion of the guy's earnings each day.

"One day the guy didn't come back, though," Sam had said. "Just took off with the money or whatever. I mean, we were kinda expecting it to happen eventually."

I didn't ask whether Sam had considered that maybe something else had happened to "their" homeless man.

After Melissa was done with her bratwurst, she offered us a gallon of what she called "wash" water, which I assumed meant it wasn't safe for drinking, so I didn't ask where it came from. John and Sam took the truck on a practice run, and the terrifying metal-on-metal grinding sound was completely gone, and the brakes were somewhat slow to stop but they worked. I couldn't believe that the grinding sound while we were driving was just from the brakes, but it was gone now, so we packed up the kids and drove Sam back to Commerce City, because the bus doesn't run on Sundays. The next week, John would pick Sam up in Commerce City, pack up everything the kid owned, and drive it to Loveland, where Sam would keep his belongings in his friend's spare closet and sleep in a hammock in a park. Within a week, he'd be sleeping on his friend's couch.

Eight

We drove to Lyons the next day to do laundry, because most of Lyric's clothing and bedding were covered in vomit. The rest of us were low on clean clothes, too, but worn clothes could be freshened up with some Febreeze. Clothes that had been vomited on were a different story. You'd think maybe I'd stop trying to force the kid to eat vegetables. Maybe I'm just stubborn.

Lyons was a town we preferred to Longmont, just a few minutes away, but there was simply never anything affordable to rent. The small town had building restrictions to prevent urban sprawl caused by developers taking advantage of the populace's desire for cheaply-rentable homes, so a limited number of homes were available. The city limits hadn't changed much in fifty years, and the city wanted to keep it that way, lest Lyons be overrun with Boulderites and Longmontians who could put a price on scenic living. Only a limited number of new homes could be built, so to move into the town, you had to be wealthy. To have an affordable home in Lyons, on the other hand, your family had to have been there for at least a generation. This preserved the attitude of the town as well, which was more progressive than Longmont but not as radical as Boulder or Nederland. The school, for example, had some of the highest-paid teachers in the nation-- It was the best-performing school in Boulder County, which has the distinction of being the most educated county in America. The art programs in the high school can't be compared to the art programs in any other public school. Private schools, in Lyons, were completely redundant to the services already provided by the public school. This, for John and I, was another draw for

Lyons. But rent was impossible.

The laundromat was in the corner of the only strip mall in town, and had floor-to-ceiling windows along one wall, which were open to let in the summer breeze. Also in the strip wall was an ice cream shop, a hair salon, and three dispensaries, so I made a brief stop while John started the laundry. Then I sat in the peaceful laundromat, switching over our clothes to a dryer and putting in an extra quarter as needed, typing away on my laptop with a pleasant high as the sunlight and breeze washed over me. John had taken the kids to the park while they waited for the laundry.

I folded all our clothes and packed them into bags, and wrote while I waited for John to return with two dirty children and a happy dog. Since I had been supposedly cooped up in the laundromat, which I hadn't minded at all, John decided we would stop and play at the creek for a while before leaving Lyons.

Lyons is a town of red-rock, with three quarries providing most of the employment opportunities in the area, aside from jobs at the school. The red sandstone is easy to break and dissolves readily in the creek, meaning the creek bed is sandy and the water is chock-full of minerals. The downside is that if you sit on the red rocks of the bank and you or the rock is wet at all, some of the rock dissolves and stains your pants red.

I sat on the rocky edge of the bank, dipping only my feet in the cool and astoundingly clear water. Sophie was a little more adventurous, and Lyric walked straight into the water, seemingly failing to notice that he was completely under the water, until much later when he was cold due to the fact that he was soaked from his hair to his clothes.

Rigby splashed around in the water and John tried to get her to play fetch, but the problem with trying to get Rigby to do dog-like activities is that she really believes she's a person. A few men in their mid-twenties floated by on inner tubes, and John and I were again painfully aware that we were only pretending to fit in with people who had leisure activities afforded to them.

We got out of the water after a bit, mostly because Lyric

was blue and his teeth were chattering, and we dried off in the sun before getting in the truck to head back to wherever. It was Monday, our usual day off, and Memorial Day anyway, so we had no real plans.

The drive from Lyons to Wal-Mart is only about seven miles on Highway 66. We were near the second mile, just out of sight from the saw-tooth ridges of the red-rock foothills behind us, when we spotted a hitch-hiker on the edge shoulder of the highway. His pack was tall; the kind reinforced with steel rods for camping. He had a dog with him and it was big. I looked at John to determine whether or not we were pulling off.

"We don't really have room," John said, looking around our truck: Rigby was between Sophie's and Lyric's car seats, and both John and I had a backpack on the bench seat between us.

"You're right," I said, and I didn't really mind.

"I need to get Rigby a pack like that," John said. I guess the dog had been wearing some kind of carrying pack, like for water and a dog bowl, but I didn't really get a good look at it.

A parking lot appeared on our right and John turned into the lot, meant for fishermen and picnickers at the nearby lake. John turned the truck around, waited for a lull in the traffic, then turned left onto Highway 66, back west towards Lyons. We spotted the hitch-hiker again, dog trotting along beside, and John turned into a farmer's driveway soon after. Heading east again towards Longmont, I watched in terror as the big, black dog darted away from the hitch-hiker; I was sure that the sedan in front of us would hit it, but the dog turned the other way, towards an open field, chasing prairie dogs playfully. Then he rejoined his master, and I realized the dog had been walking alongside his master, without a leash, the entire time. John pulled off the road in front of the hitch-hiker.

"You know, you teach the kids more about being kind to strangers when they see you do stuff like this than you ever could with a thousand lectures," I told John. He didn't say anything.

I wondered if the hitch-hiker would be afraid; he didn't know why we were pulling off in front of him, basically cutting him off between the highway and the steep ditch. But I watched in the rear-view mirror as the hitch-hiker ran full-speed towards us, dog galloping along beside. I moved John's backpack to behind John's seat and set my backpack on my lap. Then I moved to the middle of the bench seat, making room for the hitch-hiker on my right, in the passenger seat. The dog was big but I figured it'd just have to sit on its owner's lap; hopefully my impression was correct and the dog was well-behaved. I heard John exchanging the usual pleasantries and telling the man that we were going in to Longmont.

John re-entered the truck and sat in the driver's seat, then looked quizzically at the space next to me, and I looked quizzically at him. Without speaking, we both realized our miscommunication, and John shouted at the man (who was now in the bed of the truck), "Hey! Do you want to ride up front?"

"Nah, there won't be room for my dog," the hitch-hiker said.

I worried a little about them in the back of the truck on the highway, but I supposed they'd be okay; they looked pretty weather-worn as it was. And a lot of hitchhikers, the more rough-looking ones, opted for the bed of the truck anyway, even if we offered them a seat in the front. Two weeks prior, we'd driven a weathered old man down Diagonal Highway from Longmont to Boulder, and he lay down in the bed of the truck the whole way. We later saw him on Pearl Street, at a free jazz festival that was our destination.

As I slid back to the passenger side, I turned around in my seat to look at our latest hitch-hikers; The dog was a black pit-bull, larger than many I'd seen, and it grinned and slobbered in the wind. The man wore a baseball cap and had skin so dark I couldn't tell if he was perpetually sunburned or just dirty. His front teeth had a gap between them and one appeared to be chipped. Sophie and Lyric soon fell asleep, lulled by the engine on the highway and tired after their romp in the creek. Rigby was eager to meet the pit-bull, whose face was pressed against the back window, but soon grew disinterested and curled up to sleep between the children.

"How are you doing back there?" John shouted out his window when we stopped at a traffic light a few miles outside of town. The hitch-hiker must not have been having too hard of a time because he didn't offer any vocal objections.

When we got to Main Street, instead of going straight to turn into Wal-Mart at the northeast corner of the intersection, we turned right. I was worried that hitch-hiker would hop out at a stop light before I got to talk to him.

About a block south on Main, we turned into a pizza place parking lot. Join exchanged a few words with the hitch-hiker, then went inside to order a pizza. The hitch-hiker got out of the truck, but only sat on the curb of the parking lot. He lit a cigarette and his dog trotted around the parking lot. The dog had a dirty saddle-pack on, which might have once been forrest-green, and dragged a leash of indeterminable color.

I leaned out of the open truck window, and the pit bull trotted over to me, grinning in that goofy, humanoid way of which only pit mixes are capable. I leaned further to reach down and pet the dog and let him smell my hand. Rigby hopped over the seat to crawl across me and meet the pit bull. The dogs sniffed each other politely, and then Rigby started to growl. I pushed her back and stepped out of the truck, shutting the door behind me.

"Hey," I said to our hitch-hiker.

"Hey," he said. He didn't wear as many layers of clothing as the last hitch-hiker we had housed, and his pack was just as big but supported with metal poles. His jeans were patched with other parts of jeans; at first I thought it was for the extra pockets-- a butt-pocket was sewn to his right knee, and the loop and front pocket of carpenter's-style jeans were patched onto his left leg, extending from thigh to mid-calf-- but then I realized that the patches probably covered large holes in his jeans.

"Do you know if there's a Jack-In-The-Box in town?" he asked me.

"Um... I think so... There's one about half a mile south of here, on Main. I think it's a Jack-In-The-Box anyway."

"Thanks. Just curious because I have a coupon for a free burger from there."

"We could probably give you a ride down there," I said. "I'm not sure where we're going next but I'll ask John when he gets back."

"Thanks," he said. "I wanna get a burger and then I'm headed up to this abandoned house north of Wal-Mart."

"Oh yeah? The one on wheels?" I asked. The abandoned house in the empty field was supposed to serve as an advertisement for a house-moving service, which could actually pick up a house and move it off the foundation to dig a basement. Surely there were other purposes for this service as well, especially since Colorado had little purpose for basements, but I didn't know them.

"Yeah, yeah, that's the one."

"Oh yeah? John was thinking about that one," I said. He was actually interested in it as a location for our shrooms experience, but we couldn't ever find a babysitter.

"Yeah, I mean, it's not too good for kids. It's pretty dirty. But it has a mattress. So, are you guys travelers, too?"

I debated asking him if 'traveler' was a euphemism for 'homeless.'

"Nah, I mean, we don't so much any more. Last summer we traveled."

"Oh yeah? Whereabouts?"

"Mostly just here in the Rockies. Traveled all over the Rockies before we decided to settle down in Longmont."

"Where do you live now?" he asked.

"Uhh... in a broken-down motorhome in the Wal-Mart parking lot," I said, pointing across the highway. I was embarrassed this time, not because of the deplorable conditions, but because of how stable and immoveable it must seem to our new friend.

"Nice," he said, and John came back.

"It's gonna be about ten minutes on the pizza," he said. "Since we're getting it, I'm having *this*." And John reached in through the driver's side window and withdrew a joint from the coin compartment in the dashboard. He lit it, sheltered from the wind between his body and the truck, then passed it to me after a long draw. I took a hit and offered it to our hitch-hiker, who shook his head. I've never understood people who smoke cigarettes but not pot.

"How long have you been traveling?" John asked.

"About three months. I didn't have the dog pack for the first six hundred miles or so. So I had to carry all the dog food, and that sucked. My pack weighs fifty pounds by itself. So when I found the dog pack, I was like, fuck that. He can carry his own fuckin' food."

"Are you headed anywhere in specific?"

"Headed to Oregon. Started in Texas."

"Not too far left to go," I said.

"I've been in Colorado a couple of weeks now. Just came from Estes Park. I was in Boulder before that and came through here on my way to Estes."

"Why'd you leave Texas?" John asked.

"I was living with a friend and he said my dog couldn't live there any more. So I said, okay, I don't live there any more."

"Wow," John said. John always respected loyalty to a dog in a man.

"Oh, yeah, hey John. Is that fast food place on Main a, uh, Jack-in-the-Box?" I asked.

"Which one?" he replied, staring blankly.

"You know, next to the Menchies, the fast-food--"

"Munchies?"

"No, Menchies, you know, the yogurt shop..."

We eventually decided that there was probably a Jack-in-the-Box on Main, and we agreed to take our hitch-hiker there.

"I don't want to take up any more of your time," he said through the driver's side window after he hopped out of the truck bed with his dog. But he was headed back to the Wal-Mart anyway, same as us, so we offered to at least take his pack while we dropped things off at the bookstore. It'd be easier on him to walk the half-mile back to Wal-Mart without the pack, anyway.

"You guys will be there?" he asked uncertainly.

"Yeah, of course. Sure," John said, sounding like he was trying consciously not to sound like we would take off with everything this man owned. "You'll see us. We're in a Dodge Sportsman with a blue stripe. It's in the southeast corner of the lot."

"By the Panda Express," I added, hoping to be helpful.

The hitch-hiker memorized our license plate before we pulled out of the parking lot, and he was waiting for us when we returned to our RV after dropping some things off at the bookstore. We offered him some pizza, but he took his pack and his dog and he left, headed towards the abandoned house-on-wheels, and beyond it, Loveland and Fort Collins and then the state of Wyoming. I wonder still what he would have done if four complete strangers whom he had no reason to trust, and yet had trusted anyway, had stolen everything he owned. But still, others have survived with less.

Nine

I left the shop, like I did every morning, to go fill up some water bottles at the public library so we'd have clean water to drink. When I returned, John was seated at the coffee table, in deep conversation with a man named Mark Jabbour. Mark was the community college Creative Writing teacher who was at the Gail Storey event and had asked us about carrying his books. A leather briefcase was open on the counter, along with a contract. Copies of two different books written by Mark were spread on the coffee table, along with John's requisite cup of coffee. A copy of David Foster Wallace's *Infinite Jest* also lay between John and Mark, dwarfing the other two books. However, John and Mark had abandoned their business and were taking turns sipping coffee as the other made emphatic points; Mark was gesturing with the pen we usually used for contracts. I recognized the pen because it was one of my favorite Uniballs and I hoped Mark wouldn't place it in his shirt pocket by accident and take it with him.

"The thing is, all these kids come in and they think I can teach them to write. I can't. I can't put ideas into their heads. They have to have those ideas. And then we all go around the circle and read our stories and give critiques and stuff, and that's really valuable for them, but I can't teach them to write."

"You just can't teach someone to be a writer in college the way you teach someone to be an engineer," I said, eager to join the conversation.

"These kids come in and they think I'm going to make them a bestselling author or they're going to be famous. I mean, what are the odds of that? You know? I want them to just read their stories out loud, well, for one, to test the readability. For two, so they can be proud of what they wrote. That's the best I can give them."

"That's needed, though," John says. "That's what we're trying to do here. We find all these authors, and they've self-published a book-- they've *finished* a book, that's something to be proud of, and then on top of it, they've published it. They've done all the work themselves. It's something to be proud of. But instead, they're ashamed, because no one's reading it."

"The problem is that there's more writers than readers," Mark said.

"*Real* readers," John said. "People who read stuff other than Nora Roberts."

"Yeah, if every local lit author we had was also a local lit reader, then we'd be in pretty good shape," I said.

"But, I hate to say it because it's not very P.C.," Mark said, "but reading is a zero-sum game. Every time someone picks a book to read, that's time they can't spend reading a different book. Time you spend reading is time you can't spend doing something else. So quality literature doesn't always wind up at the top of the priorities list. It's a zero-sum game. Even for writers."

"Oh yeah, and there's too many writers who think that because they're writers now, they don't have to read any more. Like, they think they're done. Reading was what they did for practice before they were writers, and now that they're writing they don't need to read any more," I said.

"Oh, it's ridiculous," Mark said. "The number of people who think they can write without reading. Or the number of people who have this ideal of what a writer is, and they want to be that, without actually having to write."

"The traveling writer with no roots," John said. "The Jack Kerouac. They want to live this lifestyle."

"The Addict Writer," I said, pointing to the David Foster Wallace tome on the coffee table. "It's either The Traveling Writer or the Addict Writer."

"I've been both," Mark said, laughing.

"Oh, and you can be a traveler or an addict and still write, but people have this romanticized notion," I clarified, afraid he may have missed my point and been offended. "But there's people that don't really want to *write*. They just want to be a Traveling Writer or an Addict Writer. Just the freedom part. Just the traveling or the addiction. No work."

"Oh yeah, there's certainly some of that. This romanticized version of what a writer does. I get housewives that come in, they've been a housewife for twenty years and now they want to be a writer and write about doing the laundry or whatever. We get really old people that come in and they want to write stories about their grandma, ya know?"

"Everyone wants to feel like their life is profound," I said sadly.

"Yeah, but there's got to be some kind of filter, you know?" Mark said.

"Oh, I know. We do have a filter here, at the shop," I said. "I mean, you're a creative writing teacher, so you have some qualifications. If we don't have any connection to the author or they don't have any obvious qualifications, we ask for a review copy first."

"We actually get review copies of most of the books we carry," John added. "We review them to make sure they're up to our standards."

"Well, yeah," Mark said. "If you just carried any self-published book, that would be a whole lot of typos."

"Right?" I said. "And then someone would buy that book and, coming from our store, they would know it was self-published. And they'd see those typos, and it would undermine both the credibility of our store as well as the credibility we're trying to help self-published authors build up."

"But we don't just turn books away," John said. "We ask them to get a proofreader, or to make the cover look more professional, or whatever."

"We never turn books away on the basis of the content," I

clarified. "Just the caliber of the quality. Everything that's on our shelves has to be professional quality, no matter how weird it is."

"And that's the advantage we have over a traditional bookstore," John said. "The Big Six put out this, like, mainstream-ified junk. It's all the same. We have some weird stuff. It won't appeal to everyone. But that's the point. We don't just crank out the same templated junk that appeals to the wide unthinking masses. And, you know, better to have a few typos that have slipped by than to just be another bookstore full of *that*."

"One book we have," I said, "the author had just put an ad on Craigslist. John found it. "'Free books. Self-published. Good for taking apart to use for crafts, or for kindling.' That's what it said. This guy just had a garage full of self-published books."

"That's optimistic," Mark laughed.

"Forty-two copies to a box, and... how many boxes?"

"Stacked as high as my shoulders, taking up as much room in his garage as the size of this rug." John indicated the reddish floor rug in our seating area.

"But his book was actually under contract with a traditional publisher. I don't know who, but it was someone in the Big Six. Anyway, they wanted him to take out all the religious stuff. To make it more mainstream, right? Well, he wouldn't do it. Said that if he took those parts out, then it wouldn't be his book any more. So he self-published it instead. Never sold anything, of course. Just produced a bunch of self-published kindling"

"That's the double-edged sword," John said.

"Great thing about self-publishing," Mark said. "You might not sell anything, but you have complete control over my product. That's why I self-published this one," he said, indicating his novel on the coffee table. "Complete control over the editing, the cover. I wanted this book published the way I wanted it because I thought it was going to save the world."

"That's what I thought about my book," I said wistfully.

"That's what everyone who self-publishes thinks. It's so much work to do, you can't self-publish if you kinda sorta think it *might* be important. You gotta think it's gonna change the world. It's the only way to motivate yourself to take on a task like that. You gotta be Atlas."

"You see that a lot in self-published books," John said. "But I think we're seeing self-publishing being respected more and more."

"Hell yeah," Mark said. "It's similar to micro-brews, ya know? Twenty years ago, no one brewed their own beer."

"If you made your own alcohol, that was automatic hillbilly status," I added.

"Right? But now, lots of people do. And people respect that. It's 'craft' beer. People expect it to be of a higher quality than your Bud Light or Natty or whatever. It's less refined, a little less consistent, but it's a higher quality, a craft item. People are starting to recognize that. I think self-publishing's going the same direction, even if it's not quite there yet. It's not vanity publishing, it's *artisanal* publishing."

"Does that make the indie presses your Fat Tire?" John joked.

"We do have some really weird stuff, though," I said. "Like people that talk to dogs, and, I don't know--"

"The lady with the dead son," John broke in. "The lady talking to her dead son."

"Oh my god," Mark laughed. "That stuff *sells*. When I had my bookstore up in Evergreen, one time, we had an event with a lady whose son died when he was like ten, and she wrote this book about talking to him. It was so weird. And people showed up. By god, they showed up. So weird." I wondered if it might be the same author.

"When did you have your bookstore?" John asked.

"Man, it was right about the time of the terrorist attacks. Not a good time. Not a good time at all. I went into this strip mall in Evergreen, everyone was super wealthy, I figured it'd be easy. Twenty-two books a day. That's what I needed to sell. To pay my overhead, buy stock, and make a living. Not a good living, just my mortgage and food. I needed to sell twenty-two books a day to eat. 'That's a lot of books,' one of the distribution reps told me. And I was like, naw, it'll be nothing. Dude, I didn't sell anything. I was just hemorrhaging money. We had an event every single night-- jazz nights, spoken word nights, signings. People showed up to the events but nobody bought anything. Nobody bought a damn thing. Most of my stuff was non-fiction. I figured out, that's not what people wanted to read. They wanted their run-of-the-mill Danielle Steele and Nora Roberts and diet books."

John laughed. "That's what we need," I said. "Diet books. There's gotta be someone in Boulder."

"Did you know that the publishers lose money on most of those books? That's why they're all lookin' for the next Nora Roberts. They're losing so much money on every other book they put out and they got to find a way to make it up."

"They screwed themselves, as far as I'm concerned," I said. "They stopped finding new stories because it was easier to go with a template, so they trained their audience to prefer it that way. They trained the readers to prefer being hand-fed this baby food mush. They trained the readers to prefer mindless garbage, and in the process, they lost readers who like thinking. Now they have an audience of babies who want their baby food, and they have to keep up with the demand. They did this to themselves. They can go under for all I care. Let the audience of babies watch reality TV and sitcoms instead. Then we can stop having baby food factories masquerading as publishing companies and television sets masquerading as bookstores. Fuck 'em all. They can all go under."

"Then maybe the real bookstores can survive," Mark said, looking around the quiet room with a half-smile that suggested he was in on the scheme.

"How much did you put into your store?" John asked him.

"I put in fifty thousand and my dad put in thirty. Man, I thought I was set to go. I was writin' checks and buyin' shit... I paid for a year's lease and I lasted eight months."

"Jeez," I said. As if it was hard to believe.

"I was just bleeding money. I lost my house."

John and I tried very hard not to make eye contact at that statement.

"Do you regret it?" John asked.

"Absolutely not," Mark said, and I was relieved, for John's sake. I wondered how he'd react if anyone ever told him that yes, they did have regrets. But nobody ever answered that question the wrong way. Everyone knows the right answer to that question.

"I mean, at the time, I thought I was gonna be a bookstore owner for the rest of my life. Now, I've been a bookstore owner and a Creative Writing teacher and I've written books. I've been a Traveling Writer and an Addict Writer." He laughed. "Owning a bookstore is just something I did once."

Later, Dustin came by to discuss the upcoming release party for an anthology his press was putting out. He was wearing paint-stained jean cut-offs, hiking shoes, and a flannel shirt over a t-shirt depicting the cover of Jack Kerouac's *On the Road*. John and I had similar shirts; John's was the cover of Ray Bradbury's *Fahrenheit 451* and mine was *The Great Gatsby*. Not the blue cover with the eyes of T J Eckleburg, which I would have preferred, but a more feminine, modern cover depicting a colorful sketch of Daisy's face framed by her flapper's bob. We weren't wearing these shirts now; we just owned them. We recognized the *On the Road* shirt as being from the same company.

"When are you leaving on your adventure?" John asked him.

"Not till the end of August," Dustin said. "I have to finish up at work, and my brother's in a play the last week of August and of course I want to see that."

"We're excited for you," I said. "And we might live a little voraciously through you. We don't travel much any more, but we still pick up a lot of hitch-hikers. We're a little sad we won't ever pick you up because you won't be here."

"Maybe I'll come back to Longmont to hitch-hike," Dustin joked. "Do you have any advice for me?"

"If you have a dog, people are more likely to pick you

up," I said. "But it has to be a well-trained dog. You'll have to leave it outside if you go in anywhere that doesn't allow dogs. To get a drink at a gas station, anything. So it can make it harder, too."

"I can see that."

"Get a camper's pack. People like to pick up campers. If you look more like a camper than a hitch-hiker people will pick you up more."

"Well, who's to say what the difference is?" Dustin asked, grinning. "You sleep on the ground, you hike around. Pretty similar, to a point."

"Very true," I said. "When we were traveling last summer, we were camping for weeks at a time. We were pretty dirty. When we went in to Boulder, we liked to people-watch and play 'homeless or camping.' Like, guess whether other dirty people with a tent were homeless or campers."

"I guess the difference isn't so much how long you're on the road for," Dustin said, "but whether or not you have anywhere to go when you're done."

"I need to write that down," I said.

Before Dustin left, he bought a book; *If You Can Still Dance With It*, the book of poetry that Michael Adams left with us at the Poetry Tour.

"He's got another one out through Lummox Press," Dustin said. "I'm looking at buying that one, too. Lummox Press publishes a lot of Colorado authors. Like Jason Hardung. He's the poet laureate of Fort Collins."

"Impressive," I said. "I'll have to look into carrying his stuff."

"He's got two books," Dustin said. "One through Epic Rights Press and one through, well, Lummox." I recognized the name because Epic Rights Press published Lawrence Gladeview's latest book as well. "Jason was actually supposed to come to the Poetry Tour, but he got his license taken away and didn't have a ride."

"Oh yeah, I remember Lawrence saying something about that at the tour," I said.

"Yeah. I was actually supposed to do a reading with Jason up in Fort Collins, but then I couldn't go so Lawrence went instead. It's such a small world."

"It really is," I said, "but you know, that's what I love about you guys. There's this incredible sense of community among the poets around here. I think these sense of community they foster is just as important as the work they put out. Maybe you guys will be remembered like the other influential communities of artists and writers. Like, two separate times, I saw someone say-- I saw that poster you made for the Kleft Jaw release party, someone said that it reminded them of the Beat artists. And then I saw on a picture of Lawrence and John Dorsey from their Poetry Tour, someone commented that it reminded them of the beats, too."

"Was it a picture of them and a third guy in front of a bookstore in Boulder?" Dustin asked.

"Yeah, that's the one," I said.

"The third guy is Jason Hardung. See what I mean about a small world?"

"Yeah, exactly! I love it. It's a pretty depressing state of affairs, literature's going to hell in a hand basket with everyone reading the same Nora Roberts celebrity gossip crap. But meanwhile, you guys are creating art and supporting each others' art and making names. You're actually supporting each other's poetry, not just by showing up, but by actually buying it. You're reading what other poets are creating, and you're responding to it, and it gets a dialogue going. People are gonna look back on that and you're gonna get credit for it. If anything can save us, if anything can bring back true literature, it will be people like you."

Maybe I didn't say all that, but I should have. Dustin said something humble and he paid for his book, and we discussed the Kleft Jaw release party some more and he left.

My professed reasons for writing poetry instead of a novel

were bullshit; once I decided to write one, I took my laptop with me everywhere. I charged it at the bookstore or at the laundromat or at McDonald's, writing the whole time it charged, and then when we went back to the motorhome, I wrote until the laptop died. I've been averaging about seven thousand words a day, though I only really get a chance to write maybe every-other day.

After I charged the laptop at McDonald's, where I wrote for almost three hours while the children played and ate dinner, I decided to take the kids back to the RV and keep writing till the battery died. I don't always have this sense of urgency, that motivation, so when it strikes, I take advantage of it till it runs dry. After we returned to the motorhome, I gave Sophie my old day-planner to color in, and Lyric a stack of receipts, and I told them that if they could leave me alone and color good while I wrote until bedtime, they could have some cookies.

"I'm writing, too," Sophie said, as she wrote 'SOPHIE,' 'LOVE,' and 'MOMMY,' over and over again in on the blank pages of the calender. They were the only words she knew how to spell, and she only knew her capital letters. "I'm writing, too. We're authors. We're *both* authors."

Rigby went crazy barking, and after a minute, I realized that the long-haired man from the red Explorer with the expired tags was at our door, trying to get my attention, apparently afraid to knock on the door because it was already half-open.

"Hey, your man isn't around, is he? I was just going to ask him if I could give him a couple dollars to smoke me out before bed tonight."

"John's at work, but I'll tell you what. I'm gonna smoke tonight after I put the kids to bed. You can join me."

"That would be awesome, that would be awesome."

"You're in the red Explorer, right?" I asked.

"Yeah, but I'm parked over there." He indicated the main parking lot, east of our little alcove, towards the gigantic Wal-Mart building.

"Okay, tell you what. I don't want to leave the kids after I put them to bed. I'm gonna take them to Wal-Mart to go to the bathroom before bed, and on my way back out here I'll come get you."

"That'll work. Thank you so much."

He left and I came back inside to write. I sat back down, wanting to finish a chapter, and the kids kept coloring. I looked up a minute later and realized that the man had moved his red Explorer over to a few spaces away from our motorhome, where I could see it out the passenger window of our motorhome. It was really more of a maroon color. He sat in the driver's seat with the door open for air, like always. I kept writing.

A few minutes later, there was a knock on the side of our motorhome, and Rigby went crazy barking again. I opened it, and this time it was Melissa, the woman with the cats in the RV at the end of the alcove.

"Hey, have you seen Polar Bear around?" she asked, indicating an area behind her. Against the far end of the alcove, there was a truck whose owner she had warned me about.

"Is he the guy that lives in that truck?" I asked, pointing.

"No, Polar Bear's the one in that." She pointed to the Explorer.

"Oh, he was here earlier but I don't know where he went."

"S'alright, just wonderin'. Did that guy ever get his stuff together?"

"Who, John? My husband?"

"No, that guy... What was his name?"

"Oh, Sam. Yeah. We drove him back down to Commerce City the other day after he fixed our truck. He's got a place till the end of the month and then we're gonna help him bring his stuff up here."

"What, the end of this month or the end of next month?"

"The end of May. He's only got like another week. It's a tough situation." I meant the anticipation of homelessness once it becomes inevitable. At least we had only been forced to deal with that for forty-eight hours or so. "Hang on, what's your name again?" I asked.

"Melissa."

"That's what I thought, just wanted to be sure," I said.

"Where is your husband, speaking of?"

"He's working, he works till midnight."

"Oh, really? That's great. I didn't know he worked. That's awesome."

"Yeah, what a world we live in where you can work two jobs and still not be able to pay rent."

Then Axel appeared behind Melissa, exclaiming, "Hey, sweetheart, how've you been?" This was directed at me and Melissa excused herself, indicating that Polar Bear had returned.

"I've been alright, I've been alright."

"You guys get your truck running?" he asked, as both of the children appeared behind me. Their fondness for Axel had never decreased since the New York cheesecake.

"Yeah, yeah, Sam got the brakes fixed and then we were able to get our extra tires out of storage, so now it has tires and everything."

"Good, good, I bet that's a relief to be able to drive again."

"Sure is," I laughed.

"Well I been 'bout as busy as a three-legged cat herding turtles in a frozen pond. Thinkin' about getting rid of his one-ton." He meant his truck.

"Oh yeah?" I asked. I had never heard that expression before.

"Yeah, got a couple guys keepin' me on a retainer, it's really great. Now I can get something a little smaller for these jobs. It's great. Listen, I'm pretty busy but my friend in Canada is gonna send me my-- my stuff down. You know, my stuff."

"Oh, your writing?" I asked excitedly.

"Yeah, my writing. Listen, I been meaning to get down to your bookstore, I'm sorry I haven't yet. Been meaning to and I'll get down there soon."

"Oh, it's all right, I can't wait to read your stuff. We'll get it published." He grinned. Then, a woman pulled up behind Axel in an SUV with a large rooster perched on the edge of a dog-food bowl in her passenger seat.

"Is that a chicken?" Sophie asked, peeking around from behind my skirt.

"Yeah, it sure is," I said. Axel and the woman were talking.

"See, those are new England stripes. The grey," Axel was saying, and the woman thanked him and pulled away. Axel bid me a farewell and I went back to my writing. Nothing I could ever make up, I thought, could ever top real life. No point in ever writing fiction, unless it was just selling fact as fiction so people would read it.

What John says about the difference between fact and fiction, though, is that in fiction, you're allowed to drag your characters through hell, because you can pull them back out again. Fact sucks. You can't give your characters a successful business or a best-selling novel or even a home.

"I'm almost done with my book," I tell John when he gets home that night. "If I can write as much today as I did yesterday, then I will be done. If I finish tonight, then that's a book written in two weeks. Can you believe that?"

"Yes," he says, "But where is it *going*? What's the point?"

I look down at my laptop. "You're right," I say, embarrassed. "I should probably just scrap it all and start over."